Independently published in 2017

Copyright © Anne Veronica Hierholzer Conover, 2017

Publisher's Note

This is a work of fiction. Names, places, characters, and incidents are the product of the author's imagination or are used fictitiously, and any resemblance to actual persons, living or dead, business establishments, groups, events, or locales is entirely coincidental. Library of Congress Cataloging-in-Publication Data-Conover, Anne Veronica Hierholzer.

BOOK NAME: CLARE (2017) ISBN 9781549933455

Without limiting the rights under copyright reserved above, no part of this publication may be reproduced, stored in or introduced into a retrieval system, or transmitted, in any form or by any means (electronic, mechanical, photocopying, recording or otherwise), without the prior written permission of both the copyright owner and the above publisher of this book.

The scanning, uploading and distribution of this book via the Internet or via any other means without the permission of the publisher is illegal and punishable by law. Please purchase only authorized electronic editions and do not participate in or encourage electronic piracy of copyrightable materials. Your support of the author's rights is appreciated.

Definitions

Definitions: Clare; Latin *clarus (bright, clear...)*

CLARE

by

Anne Veronica Hierholzer Conover

Chapter 1

She stood staring at the thin wisp for the longest time, unafraid and typically curious for a five-year-old. They hovered around the customers. Soon they became a familiar curiosity to Clare Alexander that were akin to an imaginary creation of her mind were she any other ordinary child. One day she heard a whispering sound as it gently wove itself around an unsuspecting customer preoccupied with the plants and shrubs, whispering in his ear, floating about his head. They hid in a shadow, gracefully afloat upon the air.

At first, she thought maybe they were little friends that tagged along with the people, until one of these little shadows formed a face and sunk needle-sharp teeth into the head of a customer. She had never seen that before. The tiny hairs on her arms stood straight up, at the same time she sensed a suffering and darkness in the woman. Her typical child-like reaction to comfort someone who is hurt compelled her to reach out and touch the woman on the arm and before she could say "are you okay ma'am," she felt a wave of something wonderful flow through her body.

A deafening scream filled Clare's head, and the

shadowy thing came undone from the woman and repelled itself away, a look of hatred, with mouth gaping wide, lips peeled back to reveal horrid, sharp teeth, in a hideous, monstrous face. Startled, Clare's eyes widened, and her mouth shaped a silent Ohhh. She thought to herself, "Nasty mean little shadow!" Its' teeth reminded her of that day when her mom took her to the Orlando Sea Aquarium.

In the deep-water tank little silvery fishes swam in endless circles and the sharp toothed barracudas darted after them, mouths open to devour. The shadowy thing was angry at being detached from its prey. She clenched her little fists, and crossed her brow as she exuded unseen waves of her wonderfulness that captured it, and in a flash, it was extinguished. The bewildered woman sighed deeply as peace and serenity washed over her, whereas seconds earlier, her face betrayed pain, fear and anguish.

There was that time when her parents took her to church. There she was, kneeling next to her father, dressed in a pink dress that her mother made, with a wide satin bow that tied in the back. That day, her hat kept sliding back and she had to adjust it repeatedly. She knelt next to her father, waiting, as always for the altar boy to ring the bells when the priest raised a big white round wafer over his head. She wondered if the bells would come loose and bounce down the altar steps like they did last Sunday.

But they didn't come loose this time. Her disappointment in the perfect ringing of the bells turned to amazement at the gold light that surrounded the priest when he raised the big white round wafer over his head. The bells rang, the air bent a little and then something past through her body, a wonderfulness, already familiar to her. She tugged on her fathers' suit jacket and whispered, "what is that light around Father Mike?" He smiled down at his little daughter, hugged her close, his eyes filled with tears.

Her parents listened to her stories about the shadowy things, and chalked it up to childish imaginary friends and monsters. But as the years went by and the years of imaginary friends' past, the quiet gentle parents witnessed too many unexplained events to not believe that Clare was unique. She spoke out about what no one else could see to anyone who came to visit. Embarrassed, her parents took her aside and told her to speak only to them about the shadowy things, because people don't understand, and to talk about them frightened them away.

It was especially awkward when she would tell someone they had one floating near them. "There is a little shadow about your head," she would announce in her little voice. Clare knew she could make them disappear. So, ever so gently, she would find a way to touch a person, or brush up against their arm or leg such that the shadowy things would vanish.

Distressed by Clare's inability to keep quiet about the things she saw around people, her mother and father eventually stopped entertaining their friends and family at their house until she was older. They hired a companion for Clare who stayed with her when they went out for social visits. It took two weeks to find a person with whom Clare was comfortable.

One day, Madeline showed up. She told them she was looking for a summer job, and that she was going off to college in the fall. When Clare met Madeline, she smiled at her, and she liked her immediately, and it wasn't because of the pale aura that surrounded Madeline.

It was a great summer for them both. Madeline worked one on one with Clare. They took walks, made cookies, and played games. Sometimes Clare would take Madeline through the Arboretum and show her all the flowers and shrubs, pointing to this one and that one naming each as they passed. They had such fun together. Madeline grew to love Clare and Clare cried when Madeline went away to college.

Her parents admonished their daughter that no matter what, she must never tell their guests what she sees floating around their heads. She had to promise them, and she did. "No matter what, I promise I will keep the shadowy things a secret." They knew she couldn't help herself and it was inevitable that Clare would say something, and so she did, only it was more acceptable. She tapped a customer on the arm one day and said, "I have a little something for you." Then she gave them a flower, touched them, and her special energy flowed out of her and into the other person.

Clare and her parents came to an agreement that whatever she saw wrapping itself around person, that she could gently brush by that person and maybe smile at them, but say nothing to them. "Wait until the guests and relatives leave then tell mommy and daddy what you saw," her father said. They also taught her how to keep a journal and to write down or draw everything she could about the shadowy things.

Often, she would read aloud to her parents from the journal, much like any child making up a story, only Clare's stories read like horror stories. Her parents realized only a special gift could give a child such insight to illnesses and afflictions that only adults could understand. This worked well for Clare, and Clare's social development seemed to be going very well until that day at Johnston Elementary School.

Mr. Holden, the Principal of the Johnston Elementary School was a new principal in a new town. He was very excited about this job because it meant a fresh new start in a town where no one knew him. It was a fresh start together with his wife of three years and their little son. The School Administration was very impressed with his academics and his many references some from very notable people in the Chicago area where he was Principal for ten years. He came south to get out of the frigid winters. The members of the Personnel Committee all nodded in agreement as so many of them also came south to get out of the cold.

He was such a likeable guy and was well received at the reception where he met with all the teachers and gave such a wonderfully inspiring speech about education and how important it is to shape young minds and what an opportunity and challenge it was to be chosen as a school teacher. He told the story of how he had a class of delinquent students who were hardened by poverty, the streets and bad parents. He told them how he thought he could never win them over but after much determination and the grace of God it happened. By the end of the school year the kids loved him, and every child passed their exams and went on to the next grade. There were other stories too, inspiring ones that left all the teachers excited about starting a new year with a new class of students.

Two weeks before school was to start, Mr. Holden met with the parents at the first Parent Teacher meeting of the year. He gave the same speech about education and how important it was to shape young minds and what an opportunity and challenge it was to be chosen to be a parent of these beautiful young children with their innocent minds and bodies. He impressed upon the parents how important it was to be a good influence on their children to the point of sacrifice, to be a role model and example throughout their lives. It was the greatest challenge in life to raise intelligent children of good strong character.

Like the teachers, the parents fell in love with Mr. Holden, and everyone went home inspired to be a great parent. The school year was getting off to a great start. He made a point to visit all classrooms and speak to every child, asking them what their names were and what their favorite food was, and their favorite animal and favorite color and on and on. He made a point to reach out to each child and take their hand while he spoke to them, slightly stroking the top of their hand ever so gently giving them a sense of trust. He loved the way the children opened to him and spoke so freely and with such innocence!

He had such a way with children and secretly he loved the rush it gave him. That was until he came to Clare's first grade classroom. Clare was in the process of gluing a paper elephant to a piece of blue construction paper when Mr. Holden entered the classroom. Her teacher Ms. Winters, asked all the children to stand and say good morning to Mr. Holden. Clare put her glue down and stood up next to her desk. In unison, with all her classmates and in the sing song way little children announce greetings, they said, "Good Morning Mr. Holden."

He entered the class room smiling from ear to ear and with a loud and happy sounding voice said, "Good Morning Children." Clare looked up at the man dressed in a grey suit with a light grey shirt and a navy-blue tie with tiny pin dots of white sprinkled on it. It took all of five seconds for Clare to realize something was very wrong with this man with the happy voice. The air didn't feel right, like invisible mud was filling the room, she didn't like the floating shadowy thing in and out of his head, and she noticed that Mr. Holden was not in any pain, rather he seemed to be oblivious to it.

She backed up towards the blackboard and let the other children go ahead of her to greet the Principal. She noticed how he touched each child and the hair on her arms stood up straight. Finally, it was her turn to meet Mr. Holden, she was the last one in the class. She hesitated until the teacher coaxed her to come up and meet the Principal.

She came forward with her hands behind her back, hopeful that he wouldn't touch her. It disturbed her that he didn't seem hurt by the nasty thing that was now glaring and hissing at Clare as it hovered around the Principal's head. So, instead of listening to what he had to say, especially since she knew he was going to ask her the same questions he asked the other students, she just blurted out, "You shouldn't listen to that nasty shadow on your shoulder, telling you to do that bad thing to little Johnny."

She looked at the dark, smoky-gray shadow with a determined stare and a power flowed out of her. Instead of screaming and detaching itself from the Principal it bit hard into the man's head, whereby he straightened up and raised his hand as to strike her down. But he caught himself before it went too far. Like a robot he turned on his heel and left the classroom slamming the door. He immediately called her parents and set up a meeting.

Her parents dutifully came to the meeting and were horrified at what the Principal told them. "I am recommending that Clare be home schooled." He announced in his officious principal voice. "I was quite taken aback when she told me I had a shadow on me telling me NOT to do that bad thing to my son anymore, and how did she know my son's name is Johnny?!" Her parents knew the significance of what she said to him and that the reference of Mr. Holden being a pedophile was very disturbing.

Of course, Mr. Holden was very indignant and insulted that a child could possibly think like that at such a tender age. Where could she possibly have learned about such things? The implication that her parents might be involved in such behavior as to abuse their child was incentive enough to get rid of Clare and threaten her parents with a call to the County Social Services. So, her parents brought her home and home schooled her. It created quite a stir at the school and sadly her parents were looked upon with suspicion by the other parents for some time.

Home schooling Clare turned out to be the best thing they could have done for her. Besides her studies she spent a lot of time in the Arboretum working alongside her parents with the plants and shrubs and with customers. It gave her wonderful opportunities to develop people skills. She loved the customers and they loved her.

When Clare turned sixteen, her parents decided it was time for her to attend public high school, it was a good ten years after the incident with Mr. Holden. Her remarks about Mr. Holden were long forgotten by the community. The last thing that was on her mind this day, was remembering little Johnny Holden and his father.

This day, she was in a hurry to finish her breakfast before the school bus came. She wolfed down a piece of toast, and scanned the funnies and horoscope section of the newspaper.

"Oh my God!" her mother exclaimed, "Mr. Holden has been murdered!" She read aloud, "Thirteen-year-old Johnny Holden, hacked his father to death, as he slept, and then took a knife and slit his own throat." Clare's mother read on, "A suicide note was found on the kitchen table. The note described in explicit detail of how his father sexually abused him repeatedly, year after year."

Clare's breakfast seized up in her stomach, she sat in silence. Her mother began to cry, her father looked over at Clare and said, "There was nothing we could have done Clare, nothing." It was one of many times where Clare felt she failed. How could she have saved Johnny she was only a child herself. If people would just listen to her. She longed to be recognized for her special ability that helped people, but people didn't want to be helped not outright, their pride was too great, there was always a sense of shame of others finding out that they might have a problem.

She also knew how dangerous her gift would be to her if the wrong people knew about it. She kept her secret gift to herself content with anonymity as her parents taught her, but the news of Johnny Holden's death and the murder of his father weighed heavy on Clare, she still felt it was her fault, she should have done something more.

She had few friends. Her mother and father did their best to prepare her for the difficulties she would have to face in the world someday. Her home was her refuge. Where most teens were out pulling away from their parents, Clare stayed close to her family, holiday traditions, and the love they shared. She was free to be herself.

She knew everyone in her hometown, and everyone knew Clare, it didn't change the fact that she still had few friends. She did however learn to keep a closed mouth about the shadowy things. Her high school and college years toughened her up. The shadows swarmed around teens and college kids like bees to honey. It was one thing to touch a person when you are an eight-year-old non-threatening child that could smile at customers while offering them a small flower from the arboretum, at the same time, she could cast out the nasty thing in the shadow that plagued them.

But to touch someone like that in their teens and older became awkward and had too many social repercussions, sometimes she would intentionally drop a book or stumble to find a reason to make physical contact with someone plagued with a swarm of shadows. Simply brushing across their hand or touching their arm was all it took to cast them out of a teen, but it was very busy work, as shadows swirled around the teens and easily attach themselves to their victims. Going to school became an exhausting proposition.

She learned to look away. She learned to ignore them around her colleagues. She learned to interact with people as she looked down at the ground, so she would not get distracted by the hideous grins of what she knew was tormenting the person or persons with which she interacted. She earned a reputation as a very shy geek. She didn't want to know their failings, and jealousies and resentments, she didn't want to know their anger and destructive natures, she didn't want to know of their cancers, epilepsy, skin problems, feelings of ugliness, bad teeth. She didn't want to know their afflictions and temptations, secrets and sex issues.

Sometimes she would walk down the hall, crowded with between- class students clamoring with lockers, guys shouting back and forth, flirting with the girls and the girls up to their teeth in gossip and primping the best they could in ten short minutes, and Clare would bring on a glow and slight breeze as she walked the hall.

Oblivious of her gift to the students it was just a slight breeze that flirted with a strand of hair or a whiff of air around their collar but her walk down the hall caused such a supernatural raucous that she would be exhausted by the time she got to the end of the hall and her head ached from the horrid screams of the evil that hid in the shadowy things. Many easily reattached to some of the students after she passed but some kids would be given a second chance to reject a temptation. It was the least she could do.

It was a relief to move on to a college campus. By now, Clare, the shy geek had the eyes on the ground well perfected, she was very good at tuning people out. Until she ran into him at the library. He was as surprised to bump into her as she was to collide into him, arms full of books now falling open on the floor. They stared at each other. It was a force of habit to brace themselves for the swarm of shadows about the other.

They both were taken aback simultaneously, and a look of utter relief swept over their faces at the same time as they encountered an aura of pale light exuding from the other. It was the first time in a long time Clare met someone like herself. Of course, it wasn't the only time, there are plenty of people that seem to never attract the filthy things, but today she was at a loss for words. By the time she could articulate anything he smiled at her and said, "have a nice day," and walked away.

Thereafter, she returned to the library more than usual hoping to see him again. It was another two weeks before she spotted him between the stacks of books. "I can do this," she said to herself, as she got up and walked over to him.

He sensed her presence in the library again, just like the first time only now it wasn't a chance encounter it was a deliberate attempt to seek him out, she was coming up the aisle towards him, but he didn't look up, until she spoke. "Hi, I'm Clare, Clare Alexander." He looked at her and smiled. "I'm Gerry, Gerry Menderman," he said. They laughed at their silliness. They spoke briefly in whispered tones. They met later that day for coffee at the Sweet Shop, across from the

University Medical Center. Later that week he joined her for dinner. They talked for a long time.

They met in April of that year and fell in love completely. He graduated from Med School in June and his internship was in Gainesville, to begin in August. The next seven months were a whirlwind of planning for their future. Clare had another year of grad school to go before she was to return home and manage the Botanical Gardens and Arboretum. Her parents wanted to retire and travel, something they put off for years. They offered to give the Gardens and Arboretum to Clare and Gerry as a wedding gift, a gift of their blood sweat and tears of years of cultivating their business from the ground up. This was incentive enough for Clare and Gerry to settle in Marion after they got married.

The families gathered to celebrate Gerry's new practice. They announced their engagement that day and everyone cheered. The wedding was simple with only family and staff from the Arboretum who knew Clare from childhood in attendance. Their wedding took place at the Chapel of Holy Angels. Her father walked Clare up the aisle, and lovingly gave her hand to Gerry. Prisms of light from the beautiful stained-glass window that rose above the altar filtered through the chapel window and danced around the young couple at the altar. The air was light and fragrant with a sweetness that flowed throughout the Chapel. The ceremony was over all too soon.

They honeymooned in a small town in upper New York, a quiet place hidden from the glare of the big cities. For two weeks they traveled the back roads through towering pines, winding roads through small country towns, and villages until Gerry pulled into a small town in St. Lawrence County, New York, located in the Adirondack Park where two branches of the Grasse River flowed through the town.

They stayed at the Pierremont Bed and Breakfast Inn at the edge of the Grasse River in the center of the town. After they walked through the town, a small forgotten place, quiet with humble surroundings, whose population was a mere two hundred twelve people, they took a drive west on Route 27. Gerry had a surprise for Clare and was anxious to give it to her. They pulled into a gravel area off the shoulder of the road and parked the car. Off to the right was a foot path that lead into the surrounding woods and trees. They took a short walk that lead to a misty area where several waterfalls flowed into the Grasse River.

They followed the trail marked by a sign that read Lampson Falls. The air smelled fresh and clear, the pure water coming down out of the Adirondack Mountains roared past them as the waterfalls raced across the long smooth glacial stones to the jagged rocks below. They followed the Lampson Falls path that ran parallel to the river for about a quarter of a mile, across a small wooden bridge that traversed the fast-moving waters of the river, onto the opposite shoreline and continued down the small trail that dead ended at what appeared to be the backside of a farm.

Here, Gerry presented Clare with the deed to a hundred acres of farmland. "I want you to have this place. A place where you can build your own Botanical Gardens and Arboretum someday. Perhaps you could make it a place to open in the summer months when the weather in Florida is too oppressive to work. You could advertise in the nearby cities, about forty-five minutes away and for the city dwellers the drive out here would be a delightful day outing. And someday, maybe we could retire here, away from all the evil and suffering in the world. Here we can be ourselves, and not worry about someone thinking we are odd or strange or even worse, dangerous."

Clare had tears in her eyes, she never imagined for a moment that she would have a husband such as Gerry. "It's a peaceful place, that's why I chose it. It was formed in 1880 as a part of St. Lawrence County, long before you were born." He kissed her lightly on the forehead and held her close, Clare floated on a cloud of happiness.

They explored the area for two weeks. One day they came upon an Indian Reservation. They spent some time learning the history of the people that were part of Six Nations, that united numerous American Indian tribes. As they drove through the reservation, she was disappointed in the sparse development of the land and even more surprised at the sudden appearance of a Las Vegas type Casino in the middle of what appeared to be nowhere.

She was quite bewildered at the dichotomy of the wealthy Casino in undeveloped surroundings. As they headed back to the Piermont Bed and Breakfast Inn, she had a feeling of foreboding that she couldn't quite shake.

The return to Florida was way too soon, but it was time to go back to work and begin their lives together. Clare commuted the one-hour drive to Gainesville from Marion to finish her final year at the University of

Florida. Most of her work was done at in the Botanical Gardens or Arboretum so she did not have to drive in every day. Gerry was ready to open his Practice and get down to the business of Medicine. It took a lot of time to become a doctor.

Not just a doctor, but a trusted physician who was respected by his peers and who could walk the halls of a hospital and not be questioned as to what he was doing there. He had his diploma, his training, his license to practice Medicine, he followed well the protocol of the society to prepare for a career in the healing arts. He did it even though all he had to do was reach out and touch a sick person into wellness. Like Clare, he knew only too well that people regard them as freaks and quacks.

The small County of Marion, drew the winter 'snowbird' customers from the north, to wait out the frigid weather, as a result, the winter months were the most productive months for Clare's parents, renowned horticulturists, that own and operate an Arboretum and Botanical Gardens in Marion.

After she received her graduate degree from the University of Florida, she returned to Marion as a Master Horticulturist. She had a passion for harvesting healthy seeds void of any genetic alteration, growing bonsai trees and developing new hybrids, grafting roses and other blooming woody shrubs. She learned everything about plants and didn't stop with the course work at the University. Despite her extensive collection of books at home, she loved to peruse the local library for the latest books and CD's on horticulture.

She was a local celebrity of sorts, having won several awards for her hybrid blue roses, and her bonsai Dogwood tree with tiny pink dogwood flowers, and most recently her bonsai Magnolia, that bloomed tiny white flowers as fragrant as a full-size bloom.

In the greenhouse nursery she busied herself with the cultivation of new cuttings for the bonsai collection she hoped to unveil in two years. It would be a great day, advertising would be sent out, and refreshments would be offered, a class on how to cultivate, care and re-pot the bonsais would be offered. She had already been written up in the Orlando Times as Horticulturist of the Year, and enjoyed being a minor celebrity on the Channel Twelve Noon Community Hour, where she presented several 'how to' programs to the community.

The weeks and months flew by, and for their first anniversary Clare and Gerry planned a big party. Both sets of parents and many of their colleagues and friends were invited. Gerry had rounds to make early that morning and was up dressed and on his way to the hospital happy not to be on call passed noon. He pulled into Marion Memorial Hospital and parked in the "Doctors Only" parking lot. As he walked towards the hospital a sense of dread came over him. He felt heaviness in his chest as though a block of lead was weighing him down.

On the way to the hospital entrance he broke into a sweat, yet the morning air was cool. There seemed to be a delay with the elevators, so he took the stairs four flights until he reached Oncology. Using his stairwell key, he let himself onto the floor that opened to the Triage Center. As he entered the oncology ward he heard the elevator ping, and the fourth-floor elevator doors opened at the same time he entered from the stairwell.

He approached the Triage where all the patient charts are kept. Silence and emptiness greeted him. Normally, the floor was very busy with nurses coming and going. There were no patients, a day or so out of surgery, walking slowly up and down the hall. The patients were still in their beds, the beep of the cardiac machines monitored by the nurses behind the desk were silent.

He picked up one of his patients' charts, John Mallory, a recent admission who was in the late phases of stomach cancer. The air was very heavy as he headed toward his patients' room, it felt as though he was in a slow-motion dream as he slowly plodded his way down the hall. He slowly entered John's room with a cheery "Good Morning" in lieu of the odd atmosphere on the ward. John's eyes were closed as Gerry approached him. He looked down at his patient and knew instinctively how very bad this cancer was eating away at his stomach. He gently laid his hand on his chest and an undulating warmth issued forth from him and flowed easily into Mr. Mallory's body.

The patient's fragile hands began to quiver as the energy from Gerry flowed through his body. As the power grew in strength a dark shadow slowly rose up out of him. He watched as it slowly moved towards the large double window. He had seen this before, in Medical School, a dark shadow that slowly rose up out of a patient, but this one was bigger.

In fact, it was the largest embodiment of illness, sickness, evil or whatever it was Gerry had ever seen. It hovered in front of the window and slowly took form, a black sinuous limbed body stood in a threatening predatory pose, it's mouth agape as though it was about to speak, it's head hung low it's eyes set upon him.

It was unaccustomed to its extraction from a body that was nearly devoured, a soul nearly damned. It was unaccustomed to being revealed and repelled by the healing power it hated and knew so well and given to this pitiful weak man that stood before him. It took a step forward.

Gerry stood his ground, this thing that stood before him, this thing extracted from his patient, turned his stomach, a wave of illness swept over him, he broke out in a sweat as he tried to cast it out and away into some other dimension or wherever these things normally went, he never really knew where these things returned to, but he hoped this one was the furthest ever he could send it.

It slowly turned towards the window and disappeared into thin air. Gerry's heart pounded, and his breathing was labored, slowly the heaviness in his chest began to lighten up, he was racked with exhaustion. It took everything he had to banish the filth from Mr. Mallory's body.

He peered out the window down below at the parking lot. It was not banished as Gerry hoped, rather it stood in the street, very still and unseen by people passing by, it suddenly twisted its reptilian neck and head upward it's black sunken eye sockets filled with a sickly green glow and locked its glare on Gerry who felt the chill and evil bore into his head, it pointed up at him, then slowly faded away.

He was still looking down into the parking lot when he heard John speak to him, he turned around to see the man who moments before lay dying now sitting up in his bed. "Hey Mr. Mallory, how are you feeling today?" He looked like he had awakened from a good nights' sleep, his color was even and pink. John chatted happily as Gerry took his blood pressure and acted surprised at Johns' sudden wellness.

He ordered tests to assure that the healing was complete. The noises in the hall returned, the beeping life support and cardiac machines sang out in methodical high-pitched tones, the air was light, and all appeared normal again. Gerry completed his rounds with no further incidents. He had to be careful to play down the this miraculous phenomena, such that his special abilities would not be noticed or discovered, and did not draw suspicion from the medical community.

As a result, he was very careful not to heal too many people at once. Usually he went to work immediately on a patient if they first came into his office. He had more control over healing people in house, then he did at the hospital. But when patients ignored their symptoms until they collapsed on the street or in the office and were diagnosed with third and fourth stage cancers prior to their arrival at the hospital, then Gerry had to use discretion. Sometimes he would wait until loved ones brought people in, who would pray over the patients for healing. In those instances, the healing was completed at the touch of Gerry's hand and all the credit went to the One who gave him his gift.

Gerry finished up his rounds without any further incidents. He healed three more people with cancers in the first stages, the beasts he cast out disappeared immediately. The morning incident, with the horrid creature that possessed John, was on his mind. He felt ill at ease as he drove home. He tried to put it behind him, but a feeling of dread filled him. It had pointed up at him, "what did that mean?" Gerry thought to himself.

At noon he was on his way home and put the hospital events behind him. He wasn't easily frightened or a coward. But his thoughts returned to John and that filth that exuded from him. A wave of nausea settled in the pit of his stomach, and he knew, "it's too late to be afraid, it's coming after me," he thought.

Within seconds of this knowledge, this insightful thought, this, hellish knowing, the horror appeared on the hood of his car, unseen by anyone passing him on the road. Gerry's head filled with a scream as the creature came through the windshield and like a knife pierced his chest and stopped his heart.

He lurched forward grabbing his chest, his eyes rolled up into his head. At sixty-five miles per hour the car swerved onto the side of the road into a hundred-year-old Live Oak where the car spontaneously ignited, a ball of flame engulfed the car, Gerry, small birds, squirrels, chipmunks, and every other living thing in the tree. He could smell the gas and smoke and felt the heat of the flames roaring through the car as his life slipped away.

Clare was up early that morning, and had just finished up grafts to several shrubs, she was looking forward to the anniversary party, which included a feast she and her mother would prepare. Within seconds of Gerry's death, she felt the heavy twisted air that Gerry felt earlier in the morning. A cold draft preceded the beast's presence and blew through the greenhouse.

Clare sensed its' coming and Gerry's death flashed through her mind. She fell to her knees shocked by the vision of his horrid death. She dropped the branch she was in the process of grafting, and a jar full of wide rubber bands. The jar hit the floor, shattered and spilled rubber bands that rolled helter-skelter all over the concrete floor.

Her heart pounded, blood pumped through her body and made her light-headed. The beastly shadow was aware she knew it was with her. She had never seen one unattached to a human. They were always attached to someone. Instinctively she sensed this one had come for her.

She took a deep breath, and prepared herself to face what she saw in her vision of seconds past. For the first time in her life she realized the battle was for her own life and not some minor affliction that plagued a customer.

With her back to the adversary she slowly rose from the floor she reached up and grabbed the edge of the grafting table and leaned forward to steady herself. Somehow, she was not afraid, and deep down inside she felt a courage well up inside her. A warmth flowed through her veins through her muscles and pulsed through her brain, she closed her eyes as a whirl of wind past through and around her, tossing her hair all about. Then she turned to face it.

It was dark, like a deep black shadow except with depth and dimension, for a second she thought she was staring into a place deep in space, a black abysmal chasm shaped into a grin on what could be called a head. Evil attempted to bore into Clare like nothing she had ever encountered in her life.

It backed up a bit as Clare turned to face it. Its foul head averted the sight of Clare, shunned by the radiance that came forth from her. It slowly backed up and pointed to the house. Then it was gone.

In a split-second Clare heard her father shout, then her mother's blood-curdling scream. The house exploded, fire leaped through the torn roof. A ball of fire slammed the Arboretum fifty feet away breaking windows. Clare was thrown up against a planting table and fell backward onto the concrete floor. She crawled as fast as she could away from the spreading fire.

She choked on the thick smoke as she made her way out the back door just as the glass panels of the Arboretum collapsed, and shattered glass and wood into a million splinters everywhere. Her hands and face were punctured with spikes of broken glass. She staggered out and collapsed behind a large old Banyan tree that shielded her from the heat of the flames. She heard sirens in the distance, as her consciousness faded away.

Chapter 2

Clare looked out upon the grounds below her window. She couldn't help but see a different way to landscape the lawns. It was instinctive for her to visualize in her mind landscape layouts. She felt nothing as she gazed down at the grounds even though in her mind, she imagined a pleasant place to be and that place was garden.

The nurses on the floor collected funds amongst themselves and purchased clothes, shoes and a suitcase for Clare. She waited patiently for the doctor, discharge papers and prescriptions, that she was advised to take regularly, for another few months.

After months in the Marion Memorial Psychiatric Facility for long term patients, Clare was well enough to get back to work. She left Florida within days of her release. She carried nothing with her except the suitcase, and the prescriptions that she tossed in a trash can on her way out. She shipped no furniture, plants, books, or keepsakes, no clothes, personal items and treasures, as everything she cherished was incinerated by the fire.

With the deed to the New York property, and her inheritance which was stashed in a safe deposit box in the Marion County Bank, she had enough money to start over. She took a cab to the airport to catch a flight to upstate New York. She would rebuild her life far away from Marion.

She rented a room in the Pierremont Inn until she had a small building built, she made the upper floor her home. She had the first of five long greenhouses up and running, fully operational, each successive new greenhouse would be soldered together at the joints. She planned to pour herself into setting up the business then exhausted, collapse into bed at night.

That was her plan, at least and until her meds wore off which took about three days. She was determined to work through the visions, tremors and shock that still had a grip on her. "Hard work," she thought, "I just need hard work."

By the end of the first year she was in business, and as Gerry predicted on their honeymoon when he gifted her with the land, out of towners became regular customers. Her past faded slowly into a dull memory, that on occasion, would come to her in a dream when she least expected it.

The flashbacks of the fire did not fade away as the doctor said they would, with no meds to sedate her in the night, her nightmares were more and more frequent even though she fell into bed exhausted. Prior to the fire, she rarely drank. It wasn't until the disaster in Marion County that whiskey became routine. At first it was a drink after work. It wasn't so much a leisure drink before dinner it was more a drink to relax and dull the aches and pains from working outside all day, the second and third drinks were so she could sleep.

Sometimes it was all she could do to make it to the end of the day before flashes of memories taunted her. She knew she wasn't herself yet, that her strength and energy was all fouled up still. She hadn't seen a shadow hanging over a customer since the big fire in Florida.

Finally, the memory flashes taunted her throughout the day, distracting her from her work, such that by sunset all she could thing about was a drink. One night, with bottle in hand she went out and wandered her land winding her way to the place near the river, where her husband presented the wedding gift, one hundred acres of land. She groped around feeling her way to the smooth glacier rocks and sat down. She drank, talked and screamed at herself, until she passed out. Her body keeled over and slid into the icy waters of the Degrasse River, even the chill of the river didn't rouse her.

Chapter 3

Sarah and Billy Milliot argued over whether they should sell the fish they caught this morning or whether they should smoke it. "We never catch enough to make any money," Sarah said. "It just seems such a waste of time. I would much rather just keep the fish and have a fish fry with the family." "People come from the city to buy our fish at the Farmers Market, and I like selling it, I like the extra cash," Billy said. "Well we better get up a lot earlier than six o'clock in the morning to get the amount of fish it will take to make extra money, besides I don't want to clean the fish," she said.

The rush of the river could be heard from where they parked their jeep on the side of the road. Billy pulled out their cooler and fishing gear, together they untied the canoe from the top of the jeep and walked the short distance to the bank of the river with the canoe carried over head. The water was moving but not so fast that they would have to fight the current. They set their gear in the canoe and Billy pushed off from the bank into the moving current.

It was a beautiful crisp morning and for several minutes they paddled the canoe in silence listening to the chatter of the waking birds. They watched for swirls in the river where they knew fish gathered and fed. They came to the place where the smooth flat glacier rocks jutted out from the shore, a favorite place to fish especially for the large bass as they like to hide beneath the rocks. It was Sarah who spotted someone half in and half out of the water lodged between two of the large flat rocks.

They paddled over to see who it was, never expecting it would be a woman. Billy jumped out of the canoe and quickly checked to see if the woman was alive. "She is breathing but very weak. Help me get her out of the water." Sarah maneuvered the canoe as close as she could get to where the woman lay and together they pulled her over to the canoe and lifted her into it. She was unconscious, her hands and lips were blue, and her limbs were ice cold.

Sarah covered her with the blanket she always brought with her on the early spring mornings. "She stinks like booze." Sarah said. "She must have fallen in drunk. What is she doing out here in the middle of nowhere?" Billy said. They carried her back to the jeep, and set her in the back seat covered in the blanket. After they loaded up the canoe they got back on the road and headed home. "Should we take her to the Medical

Center?" Sarah asked. "We can't pay for her care if she is a bum or something like that." Billy said. "Let's take her home and see if we can bring her around."

Clare woke in a small, clean and sparsely furnished room, washed and dressed in a clean nightgown. She was sitting up that morning when Sarah came into the room to check on her. Her lips were parched, and her tongue was thick. Her hair hung in listless dull strands about her face. She had a splitting headache. "Here, sip on this it will help with the hangover," Sarah said, as she handed Clare a cup of hot liquid. She took the cup, her hands trembled as she took it, and almost spilled it on herself.

She took a sip of the hot liquid and it reminded her of chicken broth her mother used to give her when she was a child. When she would come home from school tired and sad from being made fun of by the class bullies, her mother would always have something ready for her, but the broth was her favorite comfort food. She drank it down and with shaky hands handed the cup back to Sarah.

She looked at Sarah ready to answer the obvious questions. "We found you by the River, you were drunk and passed out. We were lucky to find you when we did.

Billy and I were fishing when we came upon you. Are you new around here? We found you by the Flat Rocks at Lampson Falls," Sarah said.

"My husband bought me land that backs up to the river, as a wedding gift. I have lived in this area for about a year now. I have the new Greenhouse not far from here, it's not finished yet, and I live above the office on the property. I'm a Horticulturist, big name for a Gardner. I'm very sorry if I have put you and your husband out or been an inconvenience." Clare said. "Who would believe I'm a Master Horticulturist, who would believe anything, other than that I'm a drunk," she thought to herself.

She lowered her head and silently wept, for the first time since the fire, she wept from the depth of her being. Sarah sat on the edge of the bed, gently rocked Clare in her arms, and softly chanted in what later Clare learned was a Mohawk dialect.

She became very good friends with Sarah and Billy Milliot. They were instrumental in getting her the necessary workers to build the arboretum, greenhouses, and cultivate the gardens, and layout Clare's designs for the grounds. Clare stopped the heavy drinking and reserved it for times when the nightmares were unbearable. Each day she spent with her new friends she became more and more her old self. It would never be right, she hadn't felt the presence of her special gifts since the fire, but her strength and passion for life was slowly pulsing through her veins again.

She had little paranormal strength, in fact she hadn't seen the shadows since she left Florida. One day after she locked the greenhouse at the end of the day she found Billy waiting for her at the office door. "Come to our church tonight, we will pray with you, then you will see again." "See again?" Clare said a bit surprised and taken aback. "Yes Clare, it is time, you are strong now and it is time for you to be about the business you were born to do."

She arrived at the St. Vincent Chapel a few minutes late. The service had already started. She parked her truck and walked up the steps to the historic chapel. A large statue of a robed man holding a staff, one arm extended in welcome to all was set in a well- kept garden to the left of the entrance.

She was welcomed by the greeters at the door. Billy had been looking out for her and came down the aisle to meet her. "Come in it's almost time." Clare and Billy walked up the side aisle careful not to disturb people participating in the service. He seated Clare in the front pew and returned to his seat behind her. Soon Billy came to the front of the church and addressed the congregation. He spoke softly of a song by Jim Brickman called "Love Never Fails" He played a recording of it and Clare was surprised and comforted by the words that she knew were of a biblical origin.

> *"Love is patient love is kind*
> *Love, does not worry does not boast*
> *It is not proud, it is not rude, it is not easily angered*
> *Love keeps no record of wrongs*
> *Love never fails, never fails*
> *I promise you, my love will never fail*
> *And I will give to you*
> *Faith, hope and love.*

The recitation continued, but Clare wasn't listening, she was feeling a warmth pulse through her body and a slight wind gently teased her hair. She looked at Billy and for the first time she saw who he was. He stood at the foot of the altar, in front of the pews, chanting now in his very soft voice and he was glowing. Unlike Clare's world, Billy lived in a community that welcomed his gifts and even bestowed upon him a revered title.

Billy Running Deer Milliot, her very good friend, was known as the "Faith Keeper" of his community. Sometime into the service, Billy called Clare to the front of the church where Sarah and others came forward and laid their hands on her shoulders and back. She didn't know the Indian dialect they were chanting in, but she did recognize the energy welling up inside of her.

From that night on, her business began to prosper. At the end of the year she hoped to expand the business to include a web site, mail order plants, books and other products. On the website she called her gardens Bristol Arboretum. She built up a local clientele that continued to come from the neighboring cities and returned the following spring bringing new customers along with them, just as Gerry had predicted.

At first, she was reluctant to advertised or market her plants online or in newspaper ads. She always had a healthy group of customers. "Word of mouth is how folks find out about us," she said one day to Billy, who was now her seed buyer and business confidant. "We don't need any rough and tumble riff-raff from some far-off jungle hanging about do we?" He laughed and shook his head, "Ms. Menderman you could open more greenhouses, maybe create a chain all over the US. I just don't understand why you don't want to expand." "We're just fine the way things are, Billy." However, she finally relented and expanded the business by way of the online web site, mail orders and books, and it proved more profitable than she thought it would.

Chapter 4

She made a conscious effort to slow her ragged breathing as she sat up on the edge of her bed. She reached over and pulled a baby wipe from the plastic blue container on the bedside table and wiped the sweat from her face and neck. After a moment she got up, stepped into the shower and let the cool water pour over her from head to toe.

She stepped out of the shower and dried herself off, the rough feel of the terry cloth towel felt good rubbed against her face and body. She slipped into a clean cotton gown she made from an Egyptian cotton sheet that was too small for her bed. It was one of those situations where the wrong size was tagged on the sheet, which explained why it was on sale when she bought it, so she made it into a nightgown instead of returning it.

It was around 3:30am. Awake in the middle of the night was nothing new to Clare, sometimes she would read or when especially filled with anxiety and fear she would pray her prayers her mother taught her when she was a child. Other times she would make a cup of chamomile tea and watch TV until she drifted off to sleep, tonight she wanted a drink.

She got up and headed for the small kitchen where she poured herself a shot of whiskey and gulped it down. She did that three more times, before she made tea. She curled up in the upholstered chair near the window and looked out into the night. It was seven years since the fire. Often her nightmares were all about the explosion and death of her parents and husband.

Tonight, was no exception. After a few moments the silky-smooth calm of the whiskey took hold, numbing her mind just enough to keep the madness of the trauma of it all away, soon a deep sleepy feeling took over and Clare nodded off into a heavy dreamless sleep.

A few hours later, she squinted against the sunbeam that created a straight luminous path through the bedroom window, it was a bright sunny spring morning. She was up and dressed in ten minutes. She gulped down a cup of coffee, ate a bowl of cereal and headed downstairs to open The Bristol Arboretum. The great glass structure was built to the exact specifications of the Arboretum back home. She called it her greenhouse. To Clare it would always be simply the greenhouse.

Here, in Upper New York, she was as far away as she could get from Marion, Florida. The hundred acres farm, the wedding gift from her husband, was her home now. She felt safe here in this small, unpretentious place, hidden and remote in Saint Lawrence County, far from the main interstates that ran through upper New York State.

Her parents had invested wisely, and she was left with a hefty inheritance, Gerry's life insurance, and the insurance from the fire helped her to start a new life in New York. The trauma in Florida had become a dull memory.

Bristol Arboretum spread over seven of the one hundred acres. The rest of the acreage was in varying degrees of development. Twenty acres were in steel framed heavy glass connecting greenhouses. Another twenty acres were planted in seedling trees and shrubs with one acre set aside for the Seed Store, Office and Clare's living quarters above the Office.

It was a simple yet elegant flat that consisted of a spacious dining and kitchen area, with a mud room off the kitchen, a large living room, and to the east of the living room, were two rooms and two baths. The large flat was a replica of her home as a child. Persian carpets and fine furnishings graced the spacious rooms.

The furnishings matched each piece that vanished in the fire in Marion. The only picture of Gerry she had, she enlarged from a small two by three-inch photo that she kept in her wallet which was tucked away in the glove compartment of her truck the day of the fire. It was the only picture she had of them together, and it was taken on their wedding day, it hung over the fireplace mantel.

Smaller paintings of her parents she painted from memory, were set in frames and placed on the mantel ledge. Everything else burned that day leaving her memory to recreate as much of the beautiful life she had. Every time she remembered something of the past she acted on it and sought out whatever she could that was of a tangible nature to bring into her life.

As far as Clare was concerned she still considered herself married, even though she was widowed seven years now. A part of Clare could not move beyond that part of her past. She thought of him all the time, and mourned him every day. She felt as though he was still with her, guiding her along, alive in the air she breathed. She could love no other. Alone, yet never lonely she ran the Arboretum twelve to eighteen hours a day.

She slept well except when she had a flashback of the fire that came in the dead of night. They left her exhausted the next day, she never complained to anyone.

Sometimes Billy or Sarah would show up unexpectedly and bring a hot meal with them to share with her. It was always a comfort to have them around, but she couldn't talk with them about her past, she sensed that they already knew. So, she buried her thoughts and feelings deep down inside herself and bore the pain of her loss with a couple of shots of whiskey.

She had a steady flow of customers from nine o'clock in the morning until eight o'clock at night, nine months of the year. She closed the Arboretum in January and re-opened in March. She knew many customers by name, she was especially fond of the customers who were the first ones to come when she opened to the public.

Clare was happy. She felt good about herself, and her business here, in this peaceful place, called Bristol. In addition to growing plants, she provided shrubs and tree saplings for residential and commercial landscape designers. She kept a record of the gardens and landscapes that they built. She had a good reputation and the people loved her and she loved them.

Most people had at least one shadow hovering around them, usually they began to disappear after frequent visits to the Bristol Arboretum. Every now and then a customer would show up who suffered from a malevolent swarm that tormented them with aches and pains and that kept them on the verge of tears.

On those occasions the people that they were attached to were miserable to behold. Often pale, nervous and fidgety. Some would wear scarves to cover their bald heads from chemotherapy. Some had blood shot eyes that were glossed over. Some were over dressed, and walked about the greenhouse in an officious smirking kind of way, commenting to a fellow customer how much nicer their plants were than the ones in the greenhouse.

Some were talkers, and no matter how hard Clare tried to excuse herself, they held her in the conversation often lying, making it up as they go. Often, they would draw Clare into conversation speaking with an air of superiority trying to diminish her in subtle ways.

The liars and snotty talkers had real nasty shadows attached to them. It was hard to look at these people without being distracted by the disgusting things, their sharp little teeth sunken into a persons' neck. Always, the dark things would glare at Clare the whole time they were in her presence, as though to dare her to look at them.

On those occasions Clare would offer complimentary plants to the newcomers, they would shake her hand in gratitude, and Clare would glow that special unseen glow of hers that repelled the feign from its' victim. After a few visits, those folks always seemed a lot better.

At the end of the day, Clare would take one last walk around the greenhouse before locking up. This was her favorite time of day, as she found the walk through the Arboretum relaxing, it was the time of day she chose a segment of the grounds to inspect and went through the rows of shrubs and plants scrutinizing their growth, color and whether there was any disease on them. Mentally, she planned the next days' work schedule, while she walked, often she spoke aloud, leaving unanswered questions to no one except the plants and shrubs.

Sometimes she would talk aloud to her folks and Gerry, as though they were still alive, giving them a run down on the days' activities, and the customers she served. Clare was alone but not lonely. She rarely left the greenhouse or her place she called home above the office. Gerry seemed to be with her still, and she posed questions to his unseen self still as much in love with him now, as on their wedding day.

Tonight, she turned the final lock in the heavy glass door to the entrance of the Arboretum and immediately sensed someone behind her. She slowly turned to face a stranger, he held his hat in his hands, very still and very calm, he was about ten feet away. They looked at each other for a long moment. He was very pale but not sickly he had a kind of translucent radiance to his skin, his black hair nearly to his shoulders reflected the setting sun, he appeared thin but not too thin, eyes alert and wise. He was in traveling clothes and from the look of them he had traveled from a very cold place.

Heavy overcoat, hung open revealing a loose fitting knit jumper and dungarees turned at the cuff. Her eyes took in the wide black belt and the cuffed boots made of a faded soft leather. He reminded her of a turn of the century sailor from the north Atlantic. He seemed familiar, as though their acquaintance spanned many years. She felt safe in his presence. He must be someone she knew as a child, maybe someone who knew her parents, but she just couldn't place him.

"Can I help you, uh do we know each other? The greenhouse is closed for the night but if you let me know what you are looking for I can have it for you first thing in the morning." He continued to gaze at her, which wasn't altogether unpleasant, it was very interesting the way that he looked at her, not like other men but rather in a way that drew her in to a well of serenity that was his eyes. His face belied no emotion except and unless the otherworldly far away expression that Clare would come to regard as part of his uniqueness, could suffice as emotion. There was a long pause and finally the man spoke. "I'm Michael."

"Hoo boy," thought Clare, "maybe he's lost, perhaps a car broke down up on the road, maybe he needs money, maybe he needs food," she thought. "Okay, well Michael, I'm Clare, and let's go to my office we can talk there. I make tea this time of day, would you care for a cup?" Clare led the man to the office "Please have a seat and let me get us some tea."

She prepared a pot of tea, a tray of assorted cheese and crackers, sliced ham and several pieces of fruit. She was starved after a day in the greenhouse and couldn't help but be a bit annoyed at this sudden guest. She was tired, the sales receipts had to be recorded and the books needed to be closed out for the day. "Good grief why can't this wait 'till morning," Clare complained to herself. Despite her feelings she knew this man was different.

She sensed that he knew her, that he sought her out for a special purpose and that they shared a certain supernatural quality but his was different from hers. In a way, she felt flattered by the man, and that he deserved her attention no matter what. "So, quit your complaining dummy, and be nice," she mumbled to herself.

The man, dressed like a sailor that just came in from the rough seas, sat still as a statue, moving ever so slightly to accept a cup of tea handed to him by Clare. She set a plate of crackers, ham and a sliced apple before him. "Here you go, I'm not at my best this time of day so forgive me if I'm a little edgy," said Clare. He set his tea down and gazed at the floor while Clare ate and drank her tea.

She ate in silence, it didn't seem to matter that he wasn't hungry and continued to sit quietly apparently waiting for her to finish her meal. "I didn't realize how hungry I was!" Clare apologized, eyeing the last slice of ham and cracker. She noticed the man hadn't touched his tea or the plate of food in front of him, "Guess you're not hungry," Clare said as she looked at his untouched plate of food. She let the silence between them hang in the air for a moment before she inquired, "So what can I do for you?" "Marion, Florida, he said.

Her gut tensed, and it took everything she had to keep the nausea from turning her stomach. Her breathing quickened and her heart started to pound. The flash backs of the horrendous death of her family sped through her mind causing her to feel dizzy, she thought she would pass out. When she went pale the stranger named Michael reached over and touched her hand, now gripping the arm of the Queen Anne chair. She took a deep breath, "Marion, Florida?" she whispered. Michael spoke softly to Clare, his eyes serene and peaceful, "Calm yourself Clare."

After a moment, Clare regained her composure and when her breathing became slow and even she said, "You don't look like you are from Florida Mister, your clothes ..." yes, I know," he interrupted, "As I said it doesn't matter where I'm from, what matters is what you must do. There are others, like you Clare, who are gifted. You are not alone, and as I said, my name is Michael, not Mister."

Never in her life of almost thirty years had Clare met such a person who spoke to her this way. "What do you know of me and Marion, Florida?" "Does he know I am from there, born and raised, my folks died there, and I should have as well, somehow I survived a terrible fire," she thought to herself. "Yes," he said. "Okay, so you know what I'm thinking, what do you want?"

Michael stood up and crossed over to gaze out the window. "There is an eighty-six-year-old widow living in Marion. She bore four daughters. The widow and three of her daughters are afflicted." "What do you mean afflicted?" Clare said.
"You see people come into the store, and you see things attached to them, I believe you refer to them as those "shadowy things" a most interesting summation of these … entities," Michael said.

"So, you see them too? I can make them go away, when I encounter a customer who has one attached, but I never saw anyone with more than a few attached, a couple of nasty ones, occasionally. But the glow, soft wind, whatever it is, comes through every time.

"Yes indeed, Michael said, "a spirited breath of air, few realize from whence the gift comes. That's why I'm here. The tormented widow's life will end soon. She lives in a house that has formed an opening which is where a creature enters this world, it is a portal of death.

You have encountered this creature, it is the same one that destroyed your husband and parents seven years ago. Over several centuries the house has developed an evil presence that grows stronger every day. Many will die, and many will be claimed by this thief of souls. It cannot be destroyed it can only be sent back. I am here to help you."

"These shadows, they have a name?" Clare inquired. After a long pause, "Yes" said Michael, I believe the biblical name is …legion, separately they are referred to as minions or demons, they are the scourge of mankind. You saw something at the time of the great fire that destroyed your home and killed your parents. You have nightmares. It visits you in your dreams to remind you that it is not finished with you." "Yes, you're right, that *thing* threatens me in my dreams but at the same time it fears me, maybe because I am not afraid of it," Clare whispered.

"That thing," Michael said, "is Perditus Odium, a demon who gathers people, who by choice are ungodly. People that allow themselves to be seduced, and subsequently enslaved by their desires. Desires that leave them vulnerable to unholy spirits that want nothing more than to lead them Perditus, who wants nothing more, than to bring death and destruction to their earthly bodies, and darkness to their light bearing souls. He paused for a moment then said, "We have very little time, we must leave for Marion tomorrow."

Chapter 5

Clare insisted on closing the Arboretum until she got back from Marion. She arranged to have Bill and Sarah look after the place while she was gone. She told them she was going on a buying trip, but they knew she was lying. "We know why you are going to Marion," Billy said. "We will ride the winds and be with you in spirit." She gave them each a hug and thanked them for all they do for her. "I will be back as soon as this is done," she said.

She packed a large leather backpack with a few days' provisions and a change of clothes. She looked around the flat one last time, and locked the door. Michael was waiting for her at the truck. Still dressed in the cold weather clothing, he seemed oblivious to the warming temperatures and insisted they travel light with as little notice drawn to themselves as possible. Instead of Clare's Lincoln SUV, with all its' bells and whistles, and smooth road comfort, she decided to drive the late model Silverado even though it already had over a hundred thousand miles on it. It wasn't that the SUV might not be road worthy or an inferior vehicle, it was just that Michael was already sitting in the truck patiently waiting for her.

They drove west, then south, connecting and re-connecting on what was the most convoluted set of highways and by-ways Clare had ever had the misfortune to drive. The little towns and small cities along the way were not conducive to the needs of travelers passing through, not like the major Interstate Highways, where rest stops, restaurants and motels dotted the highways every fifty miles or so. Finally, after twelve hours, they made their way to Interstate Eighty-One going south, running parallel to the Blue Ridge Mountains.

They turned east onto Interstate Sixty-Four, and after another five hours they made their way to Charlottesville, Virginia where they stopped for the night. It was late when they checked into a motel. Michael carried her backpack to her room and retired to his room, without a word. The diner was closed for the night leaving only the motel vending machines filled with candy bars, chips, and soft drinks. After a quick meal of granola bars, chips and a bottle of water Clare showered, threw on a nightshirt and dropped into bed. She was asleep before her head hit the pillow.

Michael returned to the truck where he held vigil until dawn. The coming days would be difficult, soon, they would sense her presence and would come for her.

Morning came in the blink of an eye, at dawn Clare's phone rang. She raised up from her deep sleep and with heavy eyes squinted at the digital clock next to the ringing phone. "Hello," she said. "Good morning, this is your requested wake-up call. We wish you a good day, thank you for staying with us, and we look forward to your next visit," the recorded voice said. She did not request a wake-up call the night before, or did she, and forgot, she was so tired last night.

She dressed quickly, splashed some water on her face and was out the door and down the elevator to the lobby. She grabbed a coffee at the coffee bar, looked around for Michael, but he wasn't there. She looked out the glass doors towards the parking lot, he was in the truck, waiting for her. She wondered how he got in the truck since she was holding the keys in her hand. Seems she not only forgot that she requested a wake-up call, she apparently forgot to lockup the truck last night too.

"Good morning Michael," she said as she got into the truck. He did not speak and stared straight ahead as though he was seeing something horrible. "Not much of a morning person, are you?" She turned the key in the ignition and put the truck in reverse, she juggle a cup of coffee between hands as she maneuvered out of the parking space. She slowly drove onto the highway that led to the ramp sign, that read I-Sixty-Four East. A thunderous boom filled the air and a hot whoosh of air hit the truck which caused Clare to weave a bit as she drove away from the motel. "What was that!" She turned around just as the Lobby of the motel exploded into a ball of fire. "Drive Clare," Michael said, "drive fast and don't look back, they know we are coming. They can smell us."

"Oh God," Clare cried, "all those people inside." "Yes," Michael said, "It's too late for them." Her heart pounded in her chest, she felt as though she would faint. Gripped by a terrible fear, she tried to compose herself as she drove onto the Interstate ramp, and merged into the traffic. Her knuckles stretched white as she clung tightly to the steering wheel. She drove for two hours in silence. Finally, she pulled off the interstate to get gas, Michael said, "We have to be very quick."

Clare pulled into a busy gas station with a fast food restaurant. She drove up to pump number five. People busied about back and forth from the gas pumps to the cashier and fast food grill. An inviting aroma of coffee and bacon filled the bay area enticed customers to buy food and cup of coffee for the road.

"I have to pay the cashier first before we can pump the gas, stay here, I'll be right back. Michael looked over at her and whispered, "Don't look anyone in the eyes, keep your head down." She paid for the gas and quickly walked to the truck, Michael pumped the gas as casually as he could.

Clare wiped down the windshield and got back in the drivers' seat of the truck. The usual noise about the place faded away and it became eerily quiet. She looked around and noticed other customers pumping gas, that suddenly took an interest in her and Michael. They stopped what they were doing. As Michael hung up the nozzle four men appeared and came around the front of the number five bay and stood in front of the truck. Clare looked at the men not sure what to do until she saw a swarm of shadows around the men. They slithered through them, above them, biting them in the neck and whispering in each man's ear. The hideous things looked straight at Clare and Michael, with a deadly menacing glare.

"We got company," Clare said caught in the stare of the writhing evil that tormented each man. The men were in agony, not knowing why they were in front of the truck let alone tasting the desire for death. One man slid a credit card in the pump card slot, another unhooked the nozzle, a third man lit a match. The last two came forward and stood in front of the nozzle as the man holding the hose wet them down with the gas.

Just as Clare was about to get out of the truck and walk up to the men to banish the demonic shadows, Michael put his hand on her arm and said, "Back up Clare, now, there's too many and they are too strong for you." Michael quickly got in the truck. Clare backed away from the number five pump and turned towards the highway.

A horrid little man, his face distorted by a shadow's claw, that grabbed at his face, and that slid a long slimy tongue in the man's ear, and that bit into the side of his head, leaned into Michael's window and said, "And where do you little pretties think you're goin'?" Michael turned, and blew into the man's face, a blinding light flashed, and he staggered backward. "Now Clare! We have to go now!"

As Clare accelerated and attempted to drive away, a crowd of people ran after the truck as it screeched out of the station, and barely missed a passing car. Suddenly, the roar of fire preceded screams, followed by a deafening explosion and a scorching heat.

Chapter 6

"Sweet is the flesh I eat sweeter still is the soul I consume"

Even though Clare was still reeling from the gas station fire it didn't keep her from screaming at Michael "we could have prevented that, we could have stopped that carnage! Why didn't you do something, why didn't you help me instead of running away? What is it with you!? Are you a freakin' coward or what?" She was fuming. Michael sat quiet and waited until she finished her tirade before he responded.

"They can't know I'm with you, if they knew I'm with you, and that you know they're coming for you, it would be much worse. They want you to think these incidents are freak accidents, we have to keep going, draw as little attention to ourselves as possible," he said. She was pretty sure that whatever fight lay ahead of them was a fight she could handle, but holding back was wrong, all wrong. She never held back, she always helped and banished the shadows. Except for the disaster with her parents and husband, she always won out.

She knew she was in a state of shock, she shouldn't be driving and wondered why Michael wouldn't drive. Every few seconds her body shivered uncontrollably. She couldn't go on like this, afraid to do anything, she stared straight ahead and drove, cried and shivered. She grit her teeth and tried to remember the simplest prayer to regain her composure.

"I'm sorry you have to go through this. We are not alone, and I mean that in a good way, Clare." Michael reached over and placed his hand upon her shoulder, a sensation of peace enveloped her, a calm warmth filled her body. She felt comforted immediately, her arms and back were no longer tight with tension, her heart stopped pounding and settled to a steady beat, she took in a slow deep breath and then a calming breath passed by her.

They drove in silence for the better part of the day, they stopped only to get gas, and they got back on the road as fast as possible. Their travels through Virginia and the Carolinas was uneventful. Aside from a morning cup of coffee, Clare had not eaten anything, and it was now mid-afternoon. Michael reached behind to the backseat and pulled out some of the provisions Clare put in the back pack before they left the Arboretum.

He found fruit, some cheese and a box of crackers. He set to work cutting slices of cheese and pieces of apple to hand to Clare as she continued to drive.

He found a fresh bottle of water and opened it for her and placed it in the cup holder. They continued to drive south, rest of the afternoon they traveled through Georgia.

In an hour or so it would be dark, Clare had a headache, she was tired, travel weary, her eyes were dry and stung from the long drive. She tried to blink away the dry burn in her eyes. They were at the southern end of Georgia, and an hour away from Jacksonville, from there, they would go west to Marion. "We turn west after Jacksonville. It will be dark by then and I don't think I can drive much more. Doesn't seem to be a good idea to stop for the night either does it?" Clare said.

Michael looked at her. "Do you drive? Clare said. "I mean feel free here. I'm not the only one in the car you know." "I don't drive Clare," Michael said. "But we can pull over at the next rest stop for a bit if you need to rest. I am confident you can make it to Marion, it's just a few more hours." "Well, I'm going to need some strong coffee to get that far, there's an exit that has food symbols on it, a Micky D's is at the next exit, think I can get through the drive-in without a fireball burning us in the ass as we race away?" "Sheesh," thought Clare, "was that my bitchy self just then?" she thought. "And another thing, you have to dump those clothes. Where we're going the weather is hot, and you're going to be uncomfortable, and you'll stand out like a sore thumb, ok?"

Twenty minutes later, Clare and Michael pulled into the next Rest Area. It was lit, with clean rest rooms. She dozed off, minutes after she parked the truck. Michael stared into the darkness and listened to savage whispers, it was coming for her. He woke Clare at dawn. The evil entity was very close. She finished the coffee that she purchased the night before, and hoped for a fresh cup further down the road.

She stretched out the kinks in her muscles and joints from a sitting up, crunched position in the truck all night, and against Michaels' warning she made a quick pit stop to the ladies' room, splashed water on her face and ran a comb through her hair. She didn't hear it come up behind her, her neck snapped backwards, as something pulled her by her hair, a pain shot through her arm, the walls echoed a decided crack, and then darkness.

Chapter 7

Wedgewood Manor, 1866

Benjamin Thomas Massey, walked down the corridor of the Philadelphia Army Hospital, for the last time. His suit hung on him like a sack. He was much thinner now than when he left home for Med School. He made a point to wear the suit his parents gave him when he left Florida to attend Medical School in Princeton New Jersey.

A bright man with great energy, he was only twenty-two when he entered the College of Medicine. In three very short years, he was a full fledge Doctor of Medicine and Surgeon.

Instead of returning to Florida, Dr. Massey was recruited as an Army doctor for the North. The Civil War years shaped him into the man that now walked out of the Army Hospital, this sunny day in June, in the year 1866. An orderly, who worked alongside him in the hospital tents through the last year, carried his trunk behind him down the hall.

Dr. Massey carried a black leather bag that contained his medical supplies and instruments, an assortment of surgical tools, bandages, small bottles of common medicinal elixirs, and a marble bowl and pestle used to grind and mix medicines, a gift from his parents upon graduation from Princeton Medical College. His eyes squinted at the morning light, as he pushed open the heavy glass doors that led to the street. A carriage waited to take him to the Train Depot.

      The train ride to Savannah, Georgia proved to be uneventful, except for the recurring nightmare, every time he dozed off. The screams of the injured and dying, the smell of blood, the smell of death and rotting flesh, the piles of hacked off limbs and spilled guts, all this came flooding back every time he closed his eyes. He was told in time these dreams would fade. Until then, he had to hold on, for how long he did not know. The sheer madness of war emblazoned itself in his mind, like a bad tattoo.

      The train arrived in Savannah the next day. Dr. Massey purchased a small covered-wagon, and two horses for the trip to his newly purchased hundred acres, located in the center of the new state of Florida. It was not his intention to farm, rather, he planned to hire enough people to help grow what needed to be grown. After all, he was a doctor by trade, and would be about his profession once he got established.

Two weeks later he arrived in central Florida. The roads were hard, red clay in the dry days, and slippery, wet clay in the rainy days. Steam rolled off the Spanish moss, and rose out of the scrub and palmetto fields after a hard rain, cooling the relentless, suffocating heat that bore down on him.

At one point, the dirt roads gradually changed to a mix of sand and black earth, that revealed itself in each hoof print the horses left behind.

He drove into Marion, passed a sheriff's office, and weathered, wooden stores that sold farm equipment and foodstuffs. He passed the blacksmith barn and a saloon. Wagons loaded with supplies were parked outside supply shops, saddled horses, tethered to posts, dozed as they waited for their riders to return.

Children ran around in bare feet as their parents sold goods, shopped and traded for food and equipment. The town had an easy feel to it, the daily routine of business, and the people, made Dr. Massey feel at home. Marion was very different from the busy sophisticated thoroughfare of Philadelphia and Doctor Massey felt the nightmarish residue of war, begin to fade away.

Ten miles west of Marion, Dr. Massey came upon a sign at the edge of the road, incrusted with rust and age, it hung by one hinge. It read Wedgewood Manor, cir.1802. He turned into an overgrown road that wound through a canopy of huge live oaks, dripping with Spanish Moss. The sharp tipped Palmetto bushes, smothered the grounds in every direction.

A quarter of a mile into the property he pulled into a clearing. Surrounded by thick dense over growth, stood a burned-out shell of a home, with broken chimneys that marked the sight, at each end of the remains. War weary Dr. Massey, visualized a new home here and a new life.

He set up his medical practice near the house site, and lived there until he could afford to rebuild the Manor. He hoped to rebuild it in the southern splendor it once was, only now, it would be a place of healing, instead a place of slavery. Three years into his practice, he married Beatrice, the daughter of Michael O'Connor, an immigrant, and self- made millionaire, who mined, shipped and sold Phosphate to farmers throughout the south. He owned the Florida Phosphate Company. For the next six years Dr. Massey, Beatrice and their twin baby girls thrived.

It was a warm morning in June when the twins ran through the pasture that butted up against the white picket fence of their backyard. The sounds of a new calf echoed through the pasture. The girls ran through the pasture towards the newborn calf. It tried to stand on wobbly legs. The mother cow mooed loud as another calf dropped to the ground.

      The pasture was dotted with grey hills about a foot high like miniature grey dirt tents. It was one of these hills that the twins tripped over and fell head first tumbling over each other breaking apart the small hill. The fire ants were on them in seconds, swarmed up their legs and arms, up and over their dresses, around their neck, in their mouths, ears and hair. The girls screamed, and tried frantically to brush away the ants. They tore at their clothes to get them off. By the time someone got to them, a swarm of fire ants covered them, the bodies of both girls swelled on que in defense of the numerous bites of the fire ants, their faces and neck puffed up, and by the time Beatrice got to them, their airways were swollen shut, and the girls suffocated to death, a severe punishment for the destruction of the ant hill.

      With the tragic death of the twins a dark cloud of grief and sorrow consumed Dr. Massey and Beatrice. The reputable physician was shocked and appalled at the disaster, especially with him being a doctor, and unable to save his precious twins.

The townspeople showed up in their entirety to pay their respects to the good doctor and his wife, they brought food, and comfort. The women of the town stayed with Beatrice, and took over her responsibilities. They cared for her, and waited on her hand and foot, they oversaw the servants about their chores, and held vigil with her, until Doctor Massey finished seeing patients for the day. A shroud of inconsolable melancholy came upon Beatrice. She often wandered the house, looking for her twin girls, and many a night Dr. Massey would find his wife outside, in the dark of night, screaming and running through the pastures trying to find her children. He could not subdue her without a sedative, even then, she staggered around the house whimpering and calling the twins, calling and calling until her voice was hoarse, and she collapsed in exhaustion.

One morning, she awoke calm, and appeared to be her old self. She dressed and went down to breakfast, chatted with her husband and the house staff as though all was as it was before the death of her children. She even gave instructions to the head mistress for the day. She went to her desk and sat and prepared the days' menu, answered several letters that needed to be posted, and wrote a list of things she needed to pick up in town.

Upon completion of her morning tasks, she returned to her room, it was not uncommon for the women to rest in the middle of the day, and so she removed her day-clothes. Instead of laying down in her underclothes as was the custom, she changed into a white floor length nightgown, took her hair down, and brushed and braided it, as she did when she prepared for bed at night.

She turned down her bed. She lay down being sure her gown was arranged neatly to her ankles. Her long braided hair she arranged to fall over her right shoulder, onto her chest. She reached into the bedside table, and took out the small mother of pearl handled derringer, a 'necessary gift' her husband gave her. She was always to have it at the bedside table, in the event she was forced to defend herself from unsavory travelers, whose only vocation in life was to steal away what belonged to others, often killing those whose possessions they stole.

She examined it carefully being sure the small hand gun was loaded. She closed her eyes and for a moment her face appeared serene and peaceful, her arms folded across her chest, the derringer firmly grasped in her right hand. She thought of her daughters and remembered the sound of their voice, "Mommy where are you, please, please, please, we miss you so." "I'm coming my sweet girls, I'm coming."

A shot rang out, but no one heard it. All the servants worked three floors below. When Beatrice opened her eyes, it was dark, and her children were not there. She called to them, but there was no answer. "I'm here, I'm here," she called. "Come to me now, enough of this hiding." Only silence, and the darkness of death, greeted her. She called again and again, angry now that the children could not be found, so she screamed and screamed and ran through the darkness. She groped the walls, and felt her way from room to room.

Late that evening, after Dr. Massey said goodbye to his last patient and after he locked up the office portion of his home, he decided that perhaps, it would be a good thing to take Beatrice away for several weeks, maybe to the Wakulla Springs, in the Panhandle, west of Tallahassee. His manservant greeted him at the Manor door and said, "Missus has not come down from her afternoon rest, and she missed her afternoon Tea."

Several weeks after Dr. Massey buried his wife, the nightmares of war returned. When he awoke in the mornings he appeared exhausted, he lost weight, and was unkempt in his appearance. Some nights his manservant would find him in the living room, he stood, his hands over his ears, and moaned, "make her stop screaming, make her stop screaming I can't take it anymore." The manservant would help Dr. Massey back to bed, and sat outside his door, in order that he wouldn't wander during the night like Beatrice did.

Sometimes, late at night as the manservant would go through the house putting out the candles, and locking up for the night, he overheard Dr. Massey in conversation with someone. He indeed, carried on a conversation, often a pleasant conversation, but when he peered into the office, there was only Dr. Massey in the room.

Sometimes he would laugh, and it came to pass that the manservant understood that Dr. Massey was having a one-way conversation with Beatrice and his children. Sometimes he appeared to play a child's game, and called on Beatrice, then the children to take their turn.

It became a regular ritual in the evenings. Dr. Massey would retire to his office, where he played games with Beatrice and their children, but no one was there. Soon, the staff handed in their resignations, a steady flow of letters, piled on Dr. Masseys desk, some requested referrals for other places of employment. Dr. Massey's practice began to fail, and soon the patients stopped coming altogether. His Manservant was the last to go. The rumor about town was well known, prior to the servants' exodus who witnessed the slow demise of Dr. Massey, how Dr. Massey believed that his wife screamed incessantly through the night, and how he moaned for her to stop.

    Weeks turned to months, and months turned to years, and Wedgewood Manor fell into disrepair. Dr. Massey rarely came into town, and when he did, he looked a shadow of his old self. He spoke to no one, but whispered to himself constantly. Then, five years later, a state tax assessor came by the Manor, but found no one home. He called the Sheriff and they entered the house.

    The house was dark, mold grew up the side of the walls and a stench filled the house. They walked through the house calling Dr. Massey's name, in the hopes that he was still living here. When they reached the third floor they found a door ajar in the hall. Here they found his decomposed body, strung up in the stairwell of the attic.

For a decade Wedgewood Manor remained empty. It was rumored that passersby could hear screams in the night, that a woman in white, walked past the windows. Teenagers attracted by the spooky rumors, were the ones who reported the woman in white, as the Manor became a popular place to hang out. Sometimes, two small girls were seen on the veranda. It was reported that Dr. Massey often stood at the entrance to his road as though he were waiting for someone.

The house was bought and sold over and over through the next hundred years. Most owners who bought the Manor, didn't believe in all that ghostly nonsense. The hundred acres and house were priced lower than what it was worth, and that was all that mattered. But the owners would no sooner move in than they would be witness to the eternal routine of the Massey family, and in some cases, they saw apparitions that were the result of later residents who died in the Manor house.

In addition, there was a dark and eerie feeling of being watched, that every owner would encounter, in fact when one owner put the Manor up for sale, he told the bank that had financed his purchase of the Manor that he couldn't stand the feeling of being watched, especially in the midnight hours.

By the time Mrs. Greene bought the Manor it was well known that more than just apparitions lived at the Manor. Many people complained that every time they passed by the Manor they felt nauseas, or sick, as though they were coming down with the flu. Many people complained that their heart would begin to pound, and sheer terror would overcome them. This was especially true of the children who passed by the house. Many screamed, terrorized by something, unseen by their parents. When asked why they were frightened they said the 'black monster' was going to get them.

Mrs. Greene was a young widow, whose husband passed away, leaving her childless. She never re-married and spent thirty years running the Marion Candy Shop in town. She was a delightful woman, kind and cheery to all, especially the children, whom she dearly loved.

She was well known by all the townspeople, and as the years passed, she became an important member of the community, and after several years, became a respectable member of the Town Counsel. She resided above the Candy Store, in a small but comfortable flat, comprised of two bedrooms, a bath, kitchen, and living room.

She always wanted a place of her own, and loved the beauty and charm of the Wedgewood Manor, even though it was now considered haunted, something she didn't believe was true.

She was attentive to the sale price of the Manor and made a mental note of how much a new owner paid, each time lower than the last time. She waited patiently for the price to lower, to what she could afford. She just knew that one day, the Manor would be hers.

That day finally came, for years she saved every penny she could, and worked long hours at the Candy Store, sometimes 12 hours a day. It was a happy day when she purchased the Wedgewood Manor, in cash.

Her friends were very concerned for her, they believed the haunted house rumors, but they could not convince Mrs. Greene that it was a dangerous place to live. Even people who passed by the house to and from work every day, shared with her how they felt sick when they passed by the property.

She sold her candy store and used the money to cultivate a hundred-acre avocado grove. She hired workers to put in the grove and maintain the trees. All went well for about seven years. The groves produced an abundance of avocados that were crated up at harvest time and sent by freight train to the buyers in Atlanta, Georgia, and they sold at a very good price. Up until now, she had not experienced the first ghost.

With the success of the avocado groves, Mrs. Greene became a wealthy and well-known business woman. She loved to entertain her friends at the Manor, especially the ones that snubbed her when she was just a candy store owner. It was one of her favorite pass times.

She had restored much of the Southern beauty and grandeur that was in keeping with the original style of the Manor, and that included the little cemetery, where the Civil War doctor and his family were buried. She had it cleaned out and kept it meticulously manicured, she took great joy in telling a 'ghost story' when she took her guests on a tour of the place. It amused her to see the looks on her guests' faces, some went pale, others just looked scared to death.

She had fine taste in furnishings. One day she went up to the attic with the builder who was renovating the house, and discovered the attic was a finished fourth floor. It was a large spacious room, with long windows that allowed light to enter the entire space throughout the day. She found old toys, and discarded pieces of furniture, but her greatest find was the portraits of Dr. Massey, his wife Beatrice, and their two daughters.

There were two portraits that were hidden under a heavy dusty drape, that kept the portraits intact. The first portrait she found, was Dr. Massey's wedding day, and the second was a family portrait, that included their twin daughters. Mrs. Greene loved the portraits so much that she had them taken to a specialist, who restored them. She hung the pictures in the front room on either side of the large open stone fireplace.

She researched town records for the Massey marriage and birth certificates. She searched old newspaper articles for any information she could find about them. The more she searched, the more she realized that much of what she was finding was already known by many of the superstitious townsfolk.

The articles revealed that indeed, Dr. Massey was a civil war surgeon, who married the daughter of a wealthy business man, and that they suffered a great misfortune upon the death of their daughters, and later the death of Mrs. Massey and finally the death of Dr. Massey. She was amazed at the amount of misfortune that this poor family endured in their lifetime. All this history made for great storytelling and conversation pieces, that she would share with her party guests.

Shortly after the portraits were hung above the living room mantel, Mrs. Greene began to hear strange sounds, and see fleeting movements of apparitions that darted quickly out of her vision. Sometimes, early in the morning, just as she would begin to awaken, she felt a presence, that quickened her heart with fear and then suddenly she felt as though something, or someone had barged into her mind uninvited. She would awaken in terror.

She was too proud to admit that the townsfolk were correct, in their beliefs about the house. She was bound and determined to ignore, and dismiss the goings on in the Manor. But as the days turned to weeks, and the weeks turned to months Mrs. Greene gave fewer and fewer parties, and became more and more reclusive. Only her grove manager and a few of the groundskeepers had personal contact with her now.

She stopped coming to town. She sent a letter to the President of the Town Counsel, that stated that she decided to give up her position on the Town Counsel. After that, for months at a time, she was rarely seen or heard. People that drove passed the Manor at night, couldn't help but notice how lit up the Manor was, as though every light in the house was on, no matter the time of night. It was as though Mrs. Greene never slept or perhaps she slept during the day and worked at night.

In truth, Mrs. Greene had become more and more terrorized by the ghostly mental intrusions that took over her mind. The constant screams from the woman in white, who roamed the house all night long, the children who hovered over her while she slept, and often pushed her to the other side of the bed, pulled her sheets down, and sometimes they shook her awake, out of a deep sleep.

Sometimes, the door to the fourth floor was ajar, and when she tried to close it, she saw a man, hung by the neck, his body swayed back and forth.

Mrs. Greene no longer had a delightful, happy disposition, but rather, she was nervous, with a fearful nature, most of the time she was exhausted, and angry. The screaming woman in white unnerved her. She screamed back at her, or screamed at the children that hovered over her. She wrung her hands all the time now, and spent days at a time in her bathrobe, oblivious of her disheveled appearance, days passed before she took a bath or combed her hair. She liked being angry at the woman in white. It was as though it had become a kind of bizarre game and she plotted ways to rid her Manor of the screaming woman in white.

Beatrice's inconsolable anger opened a portal in her house, an invitation to a dark energy, that readily took up residence. A dark energy whose invitation drew entities that accumulated over the years. It was easy to torment Dr. Massey who was already wounded by the war years, a dark time in his life, that left a depression tucked away in the back of his mind. The darkness took the form of apparitions and appeared as twins, and teased the Dr. and his wife. Their sweet twins, no amount of grief and sorrow would bring back. Their mourning turned to a willing unrepentant rage and anger, fueled by evil, and so they killed themselves.

Mrs. Greene however, had no family losses, and as the current resident of the Manor, she accumulated more than one shadowy thing that swarmed and screamed in her brain, and implanted angry desires, murderous killer desires, she delighted in her psychopathic self. She no longer was the delightful Marion Candy Shop owner who loved children.

In 1945, the grove manager and field workers quit. They had not been paid in six months. The last of the avocados were sold, crated and sent to Atlanta. The money was mailed to the Manor bank account, but still the workers were not paid. With hat in hand, the grove manager called upon the widow one early morning, the field workers stood behind him in support. He was prepared to demand payment and was going to his lawyer if she didn't pay up.

His speech was well rehearsed, and he consulted an attorney in case she refused to pay them. He walked up to the great oak door with its' Lion Head brass door knocker whose eyes looked out past the grove manager. The knocker echoed through the house. He felt uneasy and awkward at having to come to the Manor like this. It was true that the widow appeared unwell, and was preoccupied with work, this he knew, as the few times he entered the house through the servants' door, in the back of the house, he could hear her scream and shout for someone to get out of her house or she would do them harm. "Who hasn't said that," he thought to himself.

He found it strange, that on several occasions when he did meet with Mrs. Greene, face to face, she was still in her night clothes, oblivious of her attire. She was dirty, and she smelled bad like someone who hadn't bathed in months! She had large dark circles under her eyes, and her eyes darted back and forth across the room, distracted by something, that he couldn't see. It was hard to get her to focus on him, and even harder for her to listen to him. He especially hated when she would stare past him, then scream, turn, and run away.

    The avocado season was finished for the year. He took this time to say goodbye to Mrs. Green, and move on to a new farm. He already sought employment at the Millwood Estate that had three hundred acres of fruit trees. Good grove managers were hard to come by, and he was hired on the spot. He just wanted paychecks for himself and his crew, and give his notice. She didn't answer the door.

    He left a letter stuck in a the crack in the door for her, that outlined the legal action he and the workers were going to take, and that he would see her in court. With that, he and the workers left Wedgewood Manor and never returned.

    That night the usual rituals of the damned were underway. The widow lay drunk on one of the downstairs davenports, passed out. It was the customary scream that woke her. She opened her eyes to the woman in white, only this time she held a torch in her hand. This agitated the widow no end, and she challenged the apparition as to who could burn the place to a crisp first!

So, she stumbled into the kitchen where she took a kitchen towel, wrapped it around a broom stick and doused it in kerosene. It lit up like a firecracker, she ran through the south end of the house chasing the apparition that was just a few feet ahead of her holding high her torch, every now and then touching the torch to a couch or table or painting or cabinet. Or so the widow thought that was what she was doing.

With torch in hand the widow ran to the front room that faced the south, and set to fire to the portraits of the Massey family, that hung on either side of the great fireplace mantel. The room was dry, and the portraits burned quickly, with the fire spreading from portrait to wall to drapes to floor and all the furnishings. The widow ran around the room setting every wall, door, nook and cranny on fire. Finally, she stood in the center of the room and watched the blaze grow. The woman in white stood near her, and for the first time ever, the woman in white did not scream, she laughed, and laughed, and laughed, it was the last thing the widow heard as she became engulfed in flames.

The firemen worked through the night to put out the fire, and keep it from spreading to the rest of the house and surrounding fields. The neighboring farms could see the blaze a mile away. The season was very dry, and it only took a single candle flame to light a fire that could spread for miles. The widows' neighbors worked alongside the firemen for hours, dousing the flames.

Finally, at dawn, the fire was under control, the south wing had completely burned to the ground. All they could do was to water down the smoldering remains of the Manor's south wing. Fortunately, the rest of the house was preserved from the fire. But the entire south wing was gone, burnt to the ground.

A blackened, charred tangle of ceiling beams and roof beams smoldered in what was once the beautiful spacious room where many parties and lively discussions about the history of the Massey family took place.

The widow's remains were found burned and blackened, it was determined that she set the fire, as the torch was still gripped in her charred hand. Since Mrs. Greene had no known relatives, the house was purchased by a group of Marion County business men, who repaired the house and cleaned up property and groves. They leased out the pastures and consigned a Tallahassee rental agency to rent out the Manor separate from the property lease. Most tenants lasted about a year, and eventually no tenants wanted to rent the house, so it became vacant. At first the avocado groves continued to produce enough fruit hat the farmer leasing the groves did well. But soon the neglect of the trees began to take its' toll and the grove contracted a disease, that wiped out every tree.

    The rumors of the widow and her encounters with the ghosts of the Manor were told repeatedly until they were legend. Despite its' history as a haunted house, and with its' long history that dated back to the Civil War era, it was determined by the Town of Marion, that it should be listed as an historic house in the state of Florida. As the years went by, the memories and legends of deaths and hauntings faded away into obscurity.

Chapter 8

In 1972, a man from Jacksonville by the name of Carl Ginsburg, bought Wedgewood Manor and its hundred acres. With a loan from Marion County Bank, Carl renovated the Manor house, and set out a new sign that read *Wedgewood Manor, circa 1802*. His wife Susan, was thrilled to own the Wedgewood Manor that is listed in the Florida Book of Historic Homes. Carl, his wife Susan, and three of their four daughters, gave the Wedgewood Manor a fresh new face. His oldest daughter Veronica, lived in Lakeland, with her newlywed husband, Daniel, a graduate student at Central State University.

In the 1970's Marion County was a thriving farming community, thousands of cultivated acres of citrus groves, peach groves, exotic plant nurseries, spanned the length and breadth of the county. It was also famous for its exclusive horse and cattle breeding farms. The community life was rich with good people, who loved interacting in social groups, that volunteered for good causes. Community festivals and fairs were well attended by people from neighboring counties. The local women were abuzz with the news that a family purchased the Wedgewood Manor which up till now was a bit of an eyesore in the landscape. They delighted in the progress of the Manor repairs, the broken and rotted fence line was torn down, and replaced with gleaming new white fences. The pastures were reseeded with Pensacola Bahia, a fine pasture grass, that was popular in the area.

Carl bought a herd of cows and a fine Hereford bull that he set out on 60 acres. He decided to farm the remaining thirty acres for produce to sell at the farmers markets in Thomasville Georgia, a short 30-minute drive from the Manor. Within five years, the Wedgewood Manor had been restored to its' former grandeur and Susan and Carl were well received by the community.

Initially, the neighbors came by to welcome the Ginsburg family with pies, preserved fruits and jellies, gallon jugs of fresh milk with two inches of pure cream on top.

The ladies invited Susan to weekly luncheons and afternoon get-togethers. It wasn't long before Wedgewood Manor and the Ginsburg's became a vital part of the community. Aside from the Manor, Susan took a special interest in the family burial plot in the east end of the property. She found two weathered grave stones with the names of Benjamin Thomas Massey, Physician, on one of the grave stones and Beatrice

O'Connor Massey on the other. The Massey family was the only complete family buried in the small cemetery. In addition, there were two small head stones now weathered and half buried in the overgrown grass, that marked graves for two children, who were born on the same day, and died on the same day. There were several other marked graves, residents of the Manor too, but void of relatives.

Susan joined the Historical Society. In her spare time researched the former residents of the Manor. The locals shared old wives' tales of the strange occurrences in the Manor house and how Mrs. Green set fire to the south wing, which is why the front entranceway of the Manor was off center to the right. The south wing was never rebuilt. Susan was delighted and intrigued to have such an interesting house. It was as though she held in her hand an historic gem with a 'haunted' element to it, which was certainly a topic for interesting conversation.

In the beginning, Susan, Carl and their daughters thrived at the Manor. His dream to have a farm was now a reality and the children were doing well there too. Now that the renovations were done, Carl decided to work through the winter months and sold grain bins for the Harvest Bin Company throughout the southeast. It meant that he'd be gone from home several days, and in some instances, he'd travel for a few weeks at a time.

It was during this time that Susan fell victim to a form of depression, which she thought came from the sleepless nights brought on by the late-night creaking sounds of the house. All old houses had creaking noises, she was told, this old house had creaky noises alright and other disturbances too, that became more and more frequent.

It wasn't long before the girls would run down the stairs exclaiming they saw 'something' standing in the hall, or someone passing by the window. One morning, Lyla had stepped out to the woodshed to gather kindling, and a few logs to build the early morning fire in the antique woodstove, before her mother got up. The wintry mornings were very dark. "It'd be helpful to have a light bulb in the shed," Lyla thought to herself...

She hung a lantern on a hook that gave enough light, such that she could see the wood pile and fill the kindling cart. It wasn't' until she turned to wheel the cart out of the shed that she noticed a man in a long coat and hat, watching her. He turned and walked away, through the roughhewn siding of the woodshed. Lyla smiled. *She* was not tormented by the ghosts of the house and *she* was not afraid.

By the time the girls were in their teens, everything seemed wrong. The girls who played joyously well together now, argued all the time. They were jealous of each other, and played bad tricks on one another. They were afflicted with bad habits and quirks that brought shame upon them. They compiled secrets. Lyla, Cayla and Marla in the teen years, nothing went right.

Lyla was accepted into a University somewhere out of state. The day came when Carl was to drive her to school and help her settle into her dorm. The car was packed, gassed up and ready to go. Everyone came out to say goodbye with hugs and kisses and promises to see her on the holidays. They waved good-bye as she and Carl drove down the long driveway to the rural route, that would take them to the main interstate.

Ten minutes later they drove back to the Manor, Lyla cried hysterically and exclaimed how she didn't want to go school after all, and could she stay in Marion and live at home, and attend college in Florida. She just couldn't leave Wedgewood. Carl was furious and walked away from her shaking his head in disgust. So much money, wasted on her, and the college out of state.

    Upon completion of her degree program Lyla took a position as a First and Second Year Science Instructor at Marion Community College, and continued to live at the Manor. Eventually, she came to believe that the Manor was her house, that it belonged to her, and no one could take it away from her. Her relationship with her parents deteriorated, especially with her father who seemed to be drawn into daily disagreements with Lyla. When their disagreements turned vicious and bitter, he threw her out of the house.

    She was banned from the Manor until his death. After much coaxing, Lyla convinced Susan to provide a small dwelling for her, a mobile home, and she lived on the property some ways out of site of the Manor for several years after her father's death, but Lyla sweet talked herself back into the Manor, with promises to care for her mother and always be there for her. Widowed and lonely, Susan relented, and let her daughter live at the Manor. It meant very much to Susan, as Lyla didn't hear or see anything of a supernatural nature, and this gave comfort to her, as she suffered many sleepless nights that left her in a state of exhaustion.

Lyla didn't hear the noises in the house. She was more intrigued at the persistence of her mothers' imaginings. For sure this meant maybe her mother was suffering from dementia, and that would mean it was just a matter of time, before she'd inherit the Manor.

At all times, Lyla had at least four or five shadows that hovered around her, in and out of her head, and filled her mind with evil thoughts and actions. She had grown into a most unpleasant, cruel person, capable of hurting people.

Her parents had raised her well, she understood social propriety and etiquette, as well as the ten commandments, that she felt, were jammed down her throat, so she kept her thoughts, actions and secrets to herself. She was a most convincing liar and her ability to commit all types of petty crimes without being caught would have put the world's best professional criminals to shame. A cruel edge, and a bold mean streak, had seeped into her consciousness of late, that she took out on her mother.

She surprised herself with the ugly mean side to herself, and she enjoyed hurting her mother, it gave her a thrill and a sense of power over her. Lately, she took to thinking of ways to kill her mother and put her out of her exhausting misery.

Chapter 9

It was another late night and Lyla sat at the bedside of her 89-year-old mother. It was a boring time in Lyla's life, she could think of so many better things to do than nurse maid an old woman. She glanced over at a family picture that hung on the wall over the fireplace mantel. Memories of her childhood came to mind. She remembered that moment the picture was taken with her sister Veronica, who stood in front of her mother, her sister's golden braids, hung loosely down her back. She remembered how she stood a few inches behind Veronica, behind the wooden lawn chair next to where her mother sat.

She remembered the thrill that went through her when she grabbed her sister's braids and pulled and pulled until Veronicas' screams alerted her mother who turned and slapped her hand to let go. She could still feel the sting of that slap, her thin dry lips grimaced at the memory. She remembered the time when Veronica was laying on her bed quietly stroking the silky fur of Puff, her mothers' beautiful white Persian cat that purred softly as it lay on Veronica's chest. Lyla crawled on the floor towards the bed and snuck up behind the cat lounging on Veronica, its' tail gently swaying back and forth.

Careful not to be seen Lyla quietly reached up to the cat, and gently pulled its' tail towards her and bit the tip of the cat's tail as hard as she could. The cat growled loudly and lunged at Veronica's face biting her nose, blood spurted everywhere. Such a funny memory, Lyla thought with a thrill of vengeance. She remembered the fight she and Veronica had, she ran through the house, Veronica whose nose was bleeding profusely now chased her down and pummeled her with her little fists tearing her blouse in the process.

It was Veronica who got punished. After all she beat up her little sister and tore her blouse. Lyla smiled, her thin-lips tightly stretched across her face, she had such a way of being the innocent one. But all this paled in favor of more recent memories.

She told convincing lies about Veronica that put darkened Veronica's relationship with her mother. Lies, that ruined visits between Veronica and her mother. Lies, that ruined Veronica's relationship with her and their younger sisters, Cayla and Marla. Lies, that made Lyla feel ever so powerful and intoxicatingly mean.

Lies weren't always successful. Sometimes they backfired. In fact, her entire career was a failure due to unsuccessful lies. But she had her ways of getting back at those who saw her lies. It was as though she had a way of wishing people dead, and coincidentally, they would sooner or later have a dreadful accident or illness. All Lyla had to do was envision them dead. Lies were what Lyla did best. They gave her pride in her 'gift'. Lying is what Lyla was all about.

Susan stirred, her eyes heavy with drugged sleep opened slowly and focused on Lyla. "They are coming for us Lyla," she said in a frail and shaky voice, "They are coming for us, and they frighten me. I want to see Father Murray, please call him to come visit. Please call him," she pleaded. "Shh, there there now Mother," Lyla said in her most soothing voice.

"Father Murray is on his way," she lied. She knew full well that he died 8 months ago. "And Veronica, I must see Veronica, where is Veronica?" Susan moaned. Lyla grit her teeth, in her most controlled voice said, "I have called Veronica many times but to no avail Mother, she just won't come here, she hates us."

At this Susan rose up from her bed, grabbed Lyla's spindly arm, and through gritted teeth, she seethed, "you lie to me, you think I don't know you lie to me, lying Lyla, that is who you are, lying Lyla!" In the blink of an eye, Lyla smacked her mother across the face, her head thrown back. "Shhhhh now mother, your time is almost here."

She lay gasping for air, her fragile cheek and jaw bones throbbed with pain, she lay with her eyes closed, her face turned away from her daughter, determined to show no pain, it was the least and bravest thing she could do, as Lyla was too strong for her and she could not fight back.

Finally, a tear gathered in her eye and slowly rolled down her throbbing cheek. "That's right mother, cry yourself to sleep now, soon this will be mine all mine, and you will no longer be here, and I will have a life!" Lyla left the room, humming as she went downstairs.

She stomped around the kitchen as was her way when angry, stiff jointed in her walk and motions. Every motion lacked fluidity and ease, rather her motions were stiff, like a robot, that moved around the room in measured steps. She grabbed a bag of chips and pulled a bottle of scotch from the cabinet and walked, like a stiff robot in need of oil in the joints, to the couch and sat down in front of the TV. Mindlessly, she shoved chips in her mouth, small pieces fell onto her lap as she crunched handful after handful. She sat there on the sofa, with a swarm of writhing shadows all around her, she stared past the inane program on the TV, all she could think about is how much she loathed her mother.

She had great plans for the Manor, if only she would die, die *die!* Oh, how anxious she was for her mother's death. She felt awash in an intoxicating state of hatred, her mind filled with sinister ways to do away with Susan. It was a busy night at the Manor in Marion, Florida. The lights flickered on and off, wraiths of every conceivable vice and temptation swarmed about Lyla, who uttered short giggles of insanity as they whispered in her ear and wriggled through her brain.

Bitter angry entities bore witness to the nights' activities. Among them were apparitions, one that looked like Beatrice, wandered the third-floor hall and screamed, apparitions that looked like her twins, faces twisted with horrid welts and decay, hovered over the sleeping old woman.

Dr. Massey stood in the corner of the Susan's room, he held his hands over his ears and moaned as Beatrice screamed and screamed. A rope hung around his neck. Mrs. Green ran through the house with a lit torch, and tried in vain to set all the walls on fire. Lyla pondered her own evil delights and obsessions, oblivious of the supernatural chaos around her.

Chapter 10

When Carl died, it was on the hottest day in August. For Carl, his death was a God-send. The misery of his failed agricultural venture was over. None of the farmers thought to warn Carl of the seven-year drought, when crops dried up in the fields. He did not believe such a thing could happen to him. He had taken out a farm loan and purchased state of the art tractors, combines and grain bins. When the crops failed, the debt could not be paid, interest snowballed until all he could pay was the interest.

After he died, Susan sold off all the equipment. She decided to keep the Manor House and the surrounding forty acres. She was lonely, and so overwhelmed at the work it took to keep the place together, that she considered a sell out and move to the Coast, a condo, in a beach town, ten minutes from doctors, groceries, churches, and volunteer opportunities. She and Carl had talked about that before he died, that maybe it was a good idea, but then they decided against it. One day, Lyla returned home with promises to take care of her, and the gardens and house.

Together they developed a "help me, help you" relationship, that Susan secretly thought would give her a measure of control over Lyla's out of control life. She hoped she could save Lyla from the misery that shrouded her and anyone who crossed her path. She hoped it would bring happiness to them both. It was the complete reverse, and it was a nightmare.

Her dreams were troubled by nightmares of regret, that hung over her like a thick black cloud, that tried to suffocate her at every breath, and it strained her weak and feeble heart. Sometimes she could not tell if she was awake or asleep, but no matter, she always knew whose voice she heard.

She recognized the voices of her three daughters just as she recognized their infant cries when they were born. A mother never forgets her child's voice. She was too weak now to call for Veronica, too late to change the direction of things. She was wrong about so many things, especially about her oldest daughter, Veronica.

Now, she lay on her bed, too weak to control her life, and she felt waves of regret flow over her. How could she have been so arrogant and proud, how could she have been so ugly, angry, and yes, jealous too. She could not control Veronica even when she lied, "you are the only one I wanted." She loved her and hated her at the same time. Somehow, she sensed that Veronica knew she lied about it.

Veronica was a dead ringer for Carl's mother, Susan's nemesis, whom she hated. When she and Carl were first married they had to live with Fiona Ginsburg, her mother-in-law, who had a propensity to catch Susan being 'bad' at every turn, and always corrected her in an oh so loving way. When she fumbled around in the kitchen, Fiona showed her a better way to cook, how to do laundry, how to care for her baby, how to clean house, always teaching and 'passing' down her traditions, but mostly she hated how Carl loved her, and was devoted to her. That she hated most.

She began to find ways to hurt Fiona and make her look bad in the eyes of her son. When Susan looked at her daughter, the exact image of Fiona, she was reminded of how much she hurt her and caused her son to choose her over his mother, who did nothing but love them both. When the phone call came from Carl's brother that Fiona passed away, she conveniently forgot to tell her husband that his mother died. Carl missed the funeral.

It took him too many years to speak up, or defend his mother to his wife, who became more and more controlling, jealous and manipulative of him. He grew to love her less and less, and lived a life of duty to raise his daughters and be a good father. The more passive aggressive and manipulative Susan became, the more Carl pulled away from her. Finally, he just learned to ignore her and found a joy and happiness with life in the country, farming and befriending the local farmers. Often, he visited Veronica who lived fifty miles away, often he stayed over a night or two to help her with the fields and gardens.

When he was alone with Veronica, he always felt wonderful unlike his time with Susan and his other three daughters. They talked badly of Veronica, the brunt of malicious jokes and mockery. Susan couldn't help herself, especially after a few drinks. She allowed herself to get sucked into the hysteria of the malicious moment as though malice had become a seductive elixir, instead of a horrible vice, and it always felt so good, the temptation was too great.

When the subject of Veronica came up, and when the other daughters were around, it always seemed so right, to engage in mean gossip, full of insults and mockery. Shamed by their behavior, Carl shook his head in disappointment, and walked away.

It didn't matter what it was, or when or where, malice always won out when Cayla, Lyla and Marla revolted against their older sister. She bore the insults in silence, which just seemed to fuel the fires of jealousy and hatred among her sisters even more. Susan always took their side no matter how wrong they were, she couldn't help herself, it felt so good, insulting jabs and verbal bullying did have its moments.

Now she lay helpless dying and consumed by enormous shame. She knew it would be over soon, but she could still think, and she could still pray even though the horrible faces came to her in her minds' eye to distract her from the prayer when she did pray. She would pray for forgiveness of her sins against her oldest daughter. She groaned slightly and as she turned her face to the wall tears of desolate regret silently rolled down her cheeks.

She desperately needed to see Veronica and ask her forgiveness. She cried out in her sleep for her confessor, Father Murray, she wanted peace and forgiveness. She knew only too well what awaited her without forgiveness. To be in the company of desolate, howling, angry souls, was not where she wanted to spend eternity.

Chapter 11

Veronica

She had a premonition, that a guest would arrive soon. As she went about her day she found herself distracted. She walked through her gardens to re-focus herself from the ominous arrival of some unknown person or persons. She wondered, "could there be more than one person on the way?"

As she walked through the gardens, she focused her thoughts on the beauty of the azaleas and their crowded clusters of blooms. Spring in Patoaka, Florida, averaged about 86 degrees and the flora was in full bloom. She hadn't trimmed the azalea bushes back in over four years and they towered over her head.

Up 'til now, she mourned her dead husband. It was time to move on, and reconnect with her natural gifts, and her duty to heal was the something she should be doing, instead of sitting around all day, or gardening, and reading. Indeed, she felt good, the ominous premonition that would soon arrive had a good vibe.

Overgrown azalea bushes lined the narrow walkway, from her home, to the chain link gate, a good fifty feet from the front door. The stunning pinks and lavender blossoms swayed as a breeze whispered through them. Butterfly bushes posed a contrast to the towering azaleas. The sun had not risen above the high tree line that bordered her property yet, and the heat of the day would not set in for another hour or so.

She sipped a cup of coffee as she walked through the gardens, and in light of the ominous premonition, today was no exception. She planned to read after her walk through the garden as always. Finally, she returned to the house, ready for the day.

Bright sunbeams cast rays of light around the room. The morning light floated above the tree line. This is where they spent so much of their 'downtime' hours. Knitting, working on the computer, reading, dreaming up places to travel and new projects to do. Overall, the house had a quiet comfortable feel to it, a simple 'cottage-like' house they bought over two decades ago.

So here they lived through good times and bad for twenty-two years. After he retired, Dan was even more productive, he finished numerous home projects that built up over the years. He painted faded walls, spruced up and remodeled this room or that one, he finished long overdue repairs and now that the house maintenance projects were done, he bought a tractor.

He was delighted in what it could do and how little time it took. It was easy to handle and turned on a dime. The tractor chugged along and made perfectly straight rows, with the plow in tow, that churned the soil. He noticed when the sun sunk below the tree line on the west side of the property, he figured he had another hour or two of daylight, enough to finish the row and put the tractor away.

A sharp pain sliced through his head and traveled down the side of his neck and lodged in the center of his chest. This would by the last row for the day he thought to himself. He suddenly felt very tired.

Veronica was in the kitchen when he fell. Dan was out turning over the soil, he had just completed a turn at the end of a field for yet another garden, when he gently toppled over like a large rag doll onto the soft pasture grass. The mower slowly drove itself into the side of the barn. That was it. His death was silent. No goodbyes, no drama, no excessive pain, just a quiet ending to a life that spanned sixty-eight years.

She ran through the field and got to him as soon as she could, but he was already gone. The Patoaka Rescue Squad pronounced him dead where he lay. She rode to the hospital in the back of the van. She insisted on taking him to the hospital, even though the med tech called his time of death in the field. She held his hand and spoke to him in soft whispers to hang on, that everything would be alright.

She waited alone in the small room, with only a few chairs and a snack machine to keep her company. The ER doctor came in and introduced himself to her. He took her hands in his and said, "Veronica your husband has suffered a major heart attack. I have just examined him and agree with the Emergency Techs that he died in the field where he fell." Great hot tears filled her eyes, and she sobbed.

The funeral was the following Tuesday. She called and left a message on the message machine at the Manor, to let her sisters and mother know that Dan died. She let them know the time and day of Dan's funeral. Only her friends, her son, Gil and his family attended the funeral. No one from the Manor even bothered to call her.

Veronica was numb with shock and grief, until she realized that he wasn't gone, not yet anyway. She caught glimpses of him out of the corner of her eye every now and then, and she took comfort in that. She knew his visits would eventually fade and she tried not to think about that either.

One morning, shortly after his funeral she stood outside and watched the rising of the early morning sun. Vivid shades of pink and orange brushed against the eternal blue of the sky, it reminded her of a passage in one of Homer's poems, it reminded her of the wonderful life she had with Dan, and how she wished time could stand still.

One night is just not enough, so Athene, Odysseus' immortal guardian, takes action to prevent rosy fingered Dawn from casting her tendrils of light across the earth. Selene's chariot must hoist the moon higher and allow the starlight to linger, leaving Dawn's horses expectant at Ocean's edge. Time stands still that night.

Until now, it had been difficult to think about the spirits at the Manor. At first, Veronica doubted their presence, eventually, she stopped talking about them to Dan or anyone for that matter, everyone thought it was great fodder for humorous conversation, and for her sisters it became another opportunity to mock Veronica and her stories of 'spirits.'

Veronica's perception of the paranormal was greater these days, was it because she lived alone? Or maybe because she's older, or maybe a little wiser, and perhaps a bit more spiritually grounded, she didn't block them out, or let them bother her anymore, especially since Dan was among them too.

Her son Gil, reminded her, had she taken time to consider moving in with him and his family yet? Of course, she couldn't say to him, "why yes, I have, but Dad is still here and until he stops coming around I really can't move anywhere. It would be so wrong to leave him here wandering around alone." Her son would have her committed she supposed. Besides, Gil was a little skittish about things that go bump in the night, like ghosts and other paranormal activity. She told him she would stay put for a few more years.

She wanted to be closer to her son, but it had to be just the right place, with some space between the houses. Something set on about two acres, newly built with no neighbors, with empty lots all around the two acres. That way if she felt it necessary, she could buy the surrounding lots before contractors got their hands on the property. She didn't want to be too close to Gil and his family, they had a right to their privacy as did she.

It just made things simpler for her. It took a lot of years to let go and not get upset or overwhelmed at the thoughts of others. Now, when she became aware of their mental activity, (it was no gift to be able to know what people think), she would say a little prayer for them and move on. Here, at home, on her twelve acres, she thrived in the silence.

She snapped out of her daydream, and put her thoughts in the here and now. She planned to drive the fifty miles to her mother's house tomorrow. She promised herself she would make a surprise visit, and spend the night. She sensed things were not quite kosher at the Manor, she could feel it. It was odd too that no one from the Manor made it to Dan's funeral.

She pondered a litany of reasons why they missed the funeral. Perhaps her mother was seriously ill, she wondered where Lyla was. Is it possible that she didn't forward the call to Marla and Cayla or even mother? If they didn't know about Dan's death, then it would be very awkward for them. Maybe the phone didn't record the message.

She knew it was useless to talk to Lyla. Usually mother got her messages and called right back. Maybe Lyla blocked the call, or just ignored it. Maybe the supernatural chaos was getting out of hand. Maybe the spirits were getting bolder and bolder. The last time she was in Marion she felt a sudden stab in her back. It wasn't the first time that 'they' touched her. The past several years now, were filled with episodes of touches, pushes, pinches and tripping.

Always some explanation was given by Susan. There was that time Veronica tripped on a puff of air as she descended the stairs in her stocking feet, and nearly fell head first into the cast iron wood stove at the bottom of the stairs. Susan simply said, "I don't know how many times I grabbed onto the banister, after I stumbled, or tripped over something on the stairs. Sometimes I think I'm just being absent-minded, why just the other day I saw nothing on the stairs and I tripped anyway."

The most surprising event was when Susan asked her to come spend a few nights with her, as Lyla planned to be out of town. She slept in her sisters' room that night. She remembered many years ago, when Gil was just a boy, they spent a few days at the Manor, and Gil slept in Lyla's room.

She remembered how he ran down the stairs, white as a sheet, he cried hysterically. Something shook him by the shoulders and scared him to death.

On another occasion, she was awakened at midnight by rough hands that squeezed and pushed hard on her neck, she couldn't breathe. She awoke to screams in her mind "Get out, get out!" She was overcome by its strength. That was the last time she slept at her mother's house.

While the Historical Society of Virginia listed Wedgewood Manor as one of the states' historic houses, no one ever toured the house. It was an inhospitable place to visit. In Veronica's opinion, Wedgewood should have been leveled a long time ago, and made into a permanent historic grave yard. For her Mother's sake, Veronica tolerated those bothersome, rude spirits that often presented themselves.

These entities were angry, and the anger, akin to fish bait, taunted the weak of spirt, until its victims succumbed to its allure of false power and the sensuality that came along with that. She also noticed how tempted she was to dislike her sisters when she was in her mother's house. The temptation was unbearable, and later she realized it was an evil entity, present among them, that hoped to bring violence between them.

Such was the case with that which took residence in her mother's bedroom. It lived in the darkness of the small closet against the window. It was hate, anger and meanness all rolled into one. She felt the nauseous presence, its ancient darkness, intent on destruction of a soul. The consequence of its' fall from grace, stripped it of the glorious light that shone within and throughout it, a fall into eternal darkness, a fall that blackened it with shame and disgrace. All this psychic knowledge came about the last time she stayed in her mothers' house.

She knew one of the entities as Perditus. It entered the house through a portal, breached by centuries of angry souls, now evil entities, disguised as lost souls that roil around in the historic Florida Manor. Such was the case with Dr. Massey's family. Legion violated them with grief, anger and depression, convinced by the whispers of sweet suicide, they perished, their souls and spirits mimicked by evil entities that cause misery and harm to the living.

The hundred plus years of evil gained power. The dark shadows planted little seeds of temptation that grew into a myriad of afflictions that like a cancer, diseased most of the minds and bodies of those who lived at the Manor. In very short order, the evil would be so great, that Perditus and his minions would be free to wander the world again, free of the confines of hell, and free to spread horrendous things upon the unsuspecting.

But now, Perditus wasn't so sure he could complete the damnation of the current resident of Wedgewood. He would however, claim three of her daughters. Despite the spiritual corruption he imbued upon Susan, she could still escape him, what with those prayers.

Those prayers would undo his damage and if she was surrounded by the right people, Perditus knew that Susan could be saved, forgiveness asked, and mercy given. He had a plan that included Lyla and Marla. They would serve as worthy allies to rid the Manor of Susan. He still had time to claim her, he had time, before Michael arrives.

Michael was coming. Of course, he would come, he always did. But he won't prevail, not this time. He would be too late this time, once the portal was fully opened, the minions would swarm and ruin all in their path. He was no match for Michael, it would take all the legion that swarmed in Wedgewood to come against him. Even then, Michael had a power to banish him. Already, at this very moment and at every turn Perditus called upon its kind to destroy Michael and that woman, Clare, as they came closer and closer.

Chapter 12

The Girls' Room

Lyla and Marla shared the same bedroom at the Manor until they were grown and on their own. Once they entered puberty, they were consumed by uncontrollable desires that left them emotional wrecks. Like writhing black snakes, shadows clung to them in mass, teen drama turned into near criminal behavior. Sexual promiscuity so consumed them, that their graduation from high school was seriously compromised.

They traded a high school diploma and graduation for drugs, pot, alcohol, group sex orgies. Both girls dropped out of school before their seventeenth birthdays. After a run with jail, bad boyfriends, several rehabs, and treatment for numerous sexually transmitted diseases, they managed to earn the GED.

The small Florida County of Marion ran out of men that did NOT know them. By the time they reached their mid-twenties they both settled for jobs at the local grocery store as cashiers, and worked for minimum wage. Over the years, anger became Lyla's middle name, she woke up angry, found reasons to remain angry during the day, and went to bed angry.

On Friday nights, she and Marla sought company in bars, but the same old guys were no longer interested in them. So, they spent the evening alone at the bar, getting drunk and passing out. On occasion, one or both of them would wake up the next day in a seedy motel room wrapped in dirty sheets, sore between their legs and no memory of how they got there or what or who they did.

Cayla was spared the life sucking affliction of addiction and promiscuity. After high school, she fell in love with herself, and her image in the mirror, along with a local boy, and married him. She planned her future and stuck to a life regimen that included completing her education, how many children she would have, the amount of weight she would gain or lose, and mostly to be better than everyone in her world. Even if she had to cheat to be the best. It was never a good day when her goals were not met.

The shadows found Cayla, possessed her, and her temptations turned to greed and vanity, that manifested itself in plastic surgery, competition to be the thinnest, or most beautiful. Her covetousness for what others had was unsurpassed. It became a stressful pursuit, and she spent so much of her energy to procure and out do anyone in looks, possessions and status, that she spent a good amount of time on a psychiatrist couch, crying, exhausted, and afraid.

Cayla suffered recurring nightmares. As she looked at herself in a mirror, she saw no face, no hair and her body, a naked blob. She took sleeping pills, so she wouldn't dream, and tranquilizers to prevent anxiety attacks, and pills to feel good about herself. As the years passed, her vanities filtered into every aspect of her life.

Her medicine cabinet overflowed with every conceivable tranquilizer, and hundreds of pills for weight, sleep, pain and happiness that alluded her at every turn. Over the years Cayla became painfully anorexic, her entire life propped up with pills and little else.

Together with her husband, it became a wicked game that was more important that life itself. Together, they were driven, driven, driven to be the best. Unbeknownst to them their behavior made them oblivious socially to the very people they coveted. The little seeds of temptation started out small and insignificant, and grew slowly until dysfunction became the norm.

Veronica was in college when her parents moved to the Manor and her sisters were sweet little girls. At first, she felt her sisters' behaviors and difficulties were par for the course in growing up. After a few overnight visits at the Manor she became aware of the ugly and sinister supernatural activity that went on there.

She tried to tell her parents that something was wrong with the house and was possibly causing problems with her sisters' ability to grow up healthy. On those occasions she was laughed at and made fun of. It was painful to watch her sisters grow into vituperative, mean women, a meanness that exuded from her sisters, like an oozing syrup, that was the farthest thing from sweet.

Generally, Veronica was good for about an hour when she visited her mother, especially when her sisters were there too. A chill emitted from their smiles that mocked and insulted Veronica in the most remarkably polite ways. She noticed that the past six months Lyla was always present, standing guard over mother, making sure that she didn't blurt out what really went on when mother and Lyla were alone.

In addition, Veronica sensed a malevolent and demonic presence in the Manor and she dreaded the thought of going there to visit her mother, and it chilled her to the bone. She felt as though it whispered to her, across the miles to stay away. Her prayers were a shield against it, and gave her the courage to face it if need be. All those years ago.

Chapter 13

The Rest Stop

Michael entered the Ladies Room at the Rest Area, enveloped in a furious, brilliant, hurricane force of light and power. The hideous demon stood its' ground, but to no avail. It roared in frustration, and a rage that reached beyond the gates of hell, where a chorus of damned souls screamed. Michael's strength overpowered the fiend, and sent it spiraling into a vacuum, that sucked it into a space, not of this world.

Silence filled the restroom. The peeled, mildewed walls, smeared with lipstick hearts, misspelled profanity and toilet graffiti was gone. Bleached white concrete block walls remained in the wake of Michaels' force of light and power. The smell of brimstone filled the room, small eddies of grey ash swirled around the floor pushed about by a slight breeze that flowed through the vents.

A cricket bravely broke the silence with a timid chirp that cued nature to resume. Fellow crickets and grasshoppers joined in, soon a morning chorus of insect life, and the early morning chatter of birds, caw-caw of crows and an occasional whooooooo of a hoot owl filled the early dawn. The early morning light reflected on the slick wet picnic tables moist with morning dew.

She lay unconscious, squeezed and doubled up underneath the sink, twisted into an impossible position. Michael reached down, pulled Clare out from under the sink. He laid her gently on her back, face up towards the ceiling, on the now pristine, clean concrete slab floor. Her neck was not broken, nor was her skull crushed, her breathing was shallow and slow.

He laid his hand on her arm and righted the broken bones, then gently lifted her into his arms and carried her back to the truck. He placed her in a sitting position on the seat, her head lolled back on the head rest. He quietly closed the truck door. He stood in front of the truck and listened to the rush of cars and trucks that sped by the rest area.

The Rest Area employees arrived and opened the Information Center. The ebb and flow of cars and trucks pulled in. Clare's truck was parked near the area that faced the woods, a picnic table was set in the shade of the trees. Behind the picnic table the air crackled and shimmered, the leaves on the trees trembled.

They didn't have much time before wraiths would break through from the abyss. They were very close now, he expected this but didn't expect Clare to be unconscious when it happened.

He knew that death would come to all at the rest area if a crack split the air and let them free. He came around the side of the truck and placed his hand on Clare's shoulder and said, "Wake Clare, we have to go now." Clare came around with a short gasp for air, as though she had been submerged underwater, and suddenly broke the surface. She took deep gulps of fresh morning air and opened her eyes. The air crackled again, this time loud enough for Clare to wince at the sound. "What's that noise?" she asked. "They are coming," Michael said, "We must go now before they break through or people will die like they did at the gas station."

The out of body experience Clare had when unconscious, flashed through her mind, she witnessed the entire incident, although unconscious, she felt an evil breath, cold and terrible upon her neck, she winced at the crack of her arm and searing pain. A dark, ancient abyss of despair and damnation bore into her mind. A force of light blinded her, a demonic roar in protest, then nothing.

She sat up and shivered. Michael removed his sea mariners' jacket and placed it around her shoulders. She scooted over to the drivers' side and started the truck. "Let's go," she said. The air crackled again this time a bulge in the air appeared behind the picnic table together with a sound of ripping metal. She backed out of the space and turned towards the interstate. The horrid scream and screeching of the damned filled her head as she drove away from the rest stop.

They crossed over the Georgia-Florida border with an hour to Jacksonville. There they would head west, for several hours then south to Marion. She knew this part of Florida well. She thought she would feel worse than she did after the trauma at the rest stop, but she only felt very hungry, and really craved a good fresh cup of coffee. They drove in silence, not because Clare had nothing to say, but because she wondered who Michael really is, it was pretty clear to her he's not the North Atlantic Mariner he appeared to be.

She glanced over at Michael, he stared ahead, his eyes scanned the highway, roadside stops and exits. She gave him a once over and said, "We really need to get you out of those winter digs Michael. A Super Center is definitely going to be our next stop." Michael looked over at her and shook his head no.

"There is very little time left, we are being followed and they must not gain on us. Any stop would be dangerous to you. In a matter of minutes, you could be killed and so would the people around you." But Clare won out, "I will be in and out of the store in a flash, especially now that they have the personal check-out counters, I don't have to wait in line. There is no way you can continue on in Florida, dressed for a winter gale off the coast of Nova Scotia!"

They drove another hour or so before they took an exit that boasted a small town with the huge blue sign that read, SUPERCENTER. Clare ran in and bought a pair of sneaks, Bermuda shorts and shirt with a tropical design and of course one's tropical attire would not be complete without a pair of Ray-Bans. She topped off the purchase with a western style straw hat.

Michael changed in the men's room. Clare smiled as he walked back to the truck. His arms and legs were fish belly white. His black hair hung shoulder length. She reached into her purse and pulled out a ponytail band. "Turn around Michael," she said. She pulled his hair behind his ears and put it in a ponytail. "There you go, now you blend in, except you need a little tan on your arms and legs!" she said. "We need to get out of here Clare," Michael said, as he glanced over at a group of bikers that slowly drove into the Super Center parking lot.

Chapter 14

The Bikers

Two weeks ago, Jake Rogers and his biker gang, paid the first and last months' rent on a large house, not far from the interstate and ten minutes from the Super Center. Scrub weeds and overgrown vines surrounded the faded green concrete block stucco home that had black mold and mildew grew up the north side.

The house was situated on fifty-acres of land, that once boasted a thriving citrus grove. After the owners passed on, their children sold the property to a developer, and rented out the house and three acres. The front door stood wide open, the air conditioner was in disrepair, and with the heat of the day flies, gnats and mosquitoes buzzed about incessantly, until they flew into one of the many bug strips that hung from the ceiling.

Inside, several women lounged around in bathrobes, they smoked dope and swilled cold beers, every now and then they checked on the children who played outside. The men were not expected until tomorrow, however they heard the roar of motorcycles in the distance, and it was the women's cue to get the place and themselves cleaned up, before their men got to the house.

They hastily ran through the house and picked up stuff strewn throughout the house, threw away trash, cleaned the kitchen, the floor awash in cans, bottles, stale and rotten food, empty cups, glasses and used drug paraphernalia. Then, they rushed to the showers where they scrubbed away the heat of the day, stale smell of booze and weed, and frantically dressed for the arrival of their men.

Jake drove into the driveway of his newly rented house. He turned his motorcycle off and put the kickstand down. His little boys, ages three and four, shouted in glee at the sight of their dad and ran out to greet him. Oblivious to the children's dirty bare legs and feet, with festering sores, he picked up the three-year-old and tossed him onto his shoulders. The child threw his head back in delight, his voice filled the air with shrieks of joy. His cherubic face was smudged with dried snot and dirt, and flies competed to settle on the green ooze that ran from his nose.

Jake grabbed the four-year-old and hoisted him onto his hip, and carried the children into the house. Within moments, Jakes' gang cruised up to the house and parked their bikes next to his. The men brushed the road dust off their jacket sleeves and pant legs, stomped their booted feet and made their way into the house. The gang had been riding all night. They robbed five Gas stations, and killed one gas attendant in the process. As usual, they covered their tracks and left no trace of their identities anywhere. It was a good haul, twenty-five thousand dollars, not bad for a nights' work.

The men were tired and hungry. There wasn't enough food to feed the small army of bikers, so Jake attached the large carry all compartment to the back of his bike, and together with several members of the gang saddled up, and rode off to the Super Center for food. The ride to the Super Center started out okay even though he was tired from an all-night drive, but something wasn't right.

He didn't feel right. He couldn't put his finger on it. Something was wrong. Then it came into him. Within seconds Jake Rogers and his gang, became demoniacs, owned and possessed, manipulated by a hoard of wraiths that whispered in their ears. Jake pulled into the Super Center parking lot, and looked around as though trying to find someone.

Clare turned the key in the ignition. Like a bell tolling, the Biker Leader turned his head in their direction. "There they are," is all he said. Several bikers had a piggy-back rider, who wore a gun or carried a rifle on the bike.

"Now Clare! We have to go now." Michael kept his eyes on the bikers, Clare's heart began to thump in her chest as the full impact of a possible shoot out in the Super Center parking lot took hold. "You don't have to say it twice!" Clare was not ready for another fight, she was tired and hungry, and the bikers were moving in their direction.

She drove as fast as she could back to the interstate. She could hear the roar of the bikers behind her, she glanced in her rear-view mirror, the bikers were about a quarter of a mile behind and gaining. She accelerated to eighty miles per hour hoping to out run them. They pulled ahead and for a moment it seemed she left the bikers in the dust. Then she could hear the roar of the bikes, faintly behind her, she glanced out the rear-view mirror, the bikers were coming up on the left-hand lane, fast, guns drawn.

"This is not good," Clare said, "what in the world are we going to do? They are gaining on us!" "Just drive Clare and don't take your eyes off the road, no matter what you hear or see. Keep it steady, go no faster than you are now," directed Michael in a calm voice. Clare's knuckles were white on the steering wheel. In the corner of her eye she could see the bikers coming closer changing lanes and returning to the fast lane to drive as close to the truck as possible.

Soon the bikers were close enough for Clare to see the twisted hatred deforming their faces and eyes wide with something not of this world. Michael climbed out the passenger side window and adeptly flipped himself into the bed of the truck. He waited until the bikers were even with them, then opened his mouth and let loose a powerful utterance that blasted the air and rattled Clare to her very bones.

Eyes glued to the road, her hands shook on the steering wheel, her heart pounded in her chest. It seemed like an eternity, the sound blasted out from the back of the truck, but it was only a few seconds, it reminded her of a show she watched on NOVA, a documentary on the life cycle of whales and the way they communicated with each other. A diver could be pushed through the water at the song of a singing whale as the force of its song would exude intense pressure. Suddenly everything seemed as though it was in slow motion, she looked out her window just in time to see the bikers and their bikes lift off the highway and land in the median that separates the east bound lane from the west bound lane tumbling head over heels amongst the sharp pointy leafed palmetto bushes and pine trees. All this occurred during the blast of sound that came forth from Michael in the back of the truck.

In an instant it was over, and it was highway business as usual. Clare slowed to seventy miles per hour, still traumatized and not so sure that what she saw could be true. She glanced in the rear-view mirror and the bikers were out of sight. It would be awhile before they had all their bike parts picked up and put back together again, let alone the broken body parts that would have to be mended. "That should slow them" she said to herself. She tried to focus on the next leg of the trip and not think about the past few days.

She felt her courage ebb, terror creeped into her. Even when the Arboretum was destroyed and in the presence of that hideous evil, it seems more dangerous now, what with the recent events, she dared not think of what's to come. Deep down inside, ever since her parents and husband were taken from her, she knew she could hold her own on a psychic level any day of the week. Just maybe not today. She needed to pull over, because she realized that what she was feeling wasn't so much fear as good old-fashioned shock, and she was going to close her eyes any moment now, and pass out.

She pulled over to the shoulder of the road, cars and trucks zoomed past. She leaned back in her seat, her head lolled over on her chest. Michael came around and sat in the front seat. He let her rest and patiently waited for her to wake. Only a few miles to go before they turned towards Marion.

The air crackled around them. An invisible wall separated the legion of evil that sought them and humanity. Through his eyes they were visible, he watched as they pressed against the transparent wall, pushing to break through. They dare not break the barrier in his presence. They knew him all too well.

They pushed and pressed against the transparent wall, a warning that they would get Clare one way or the other. He couldn't protect her all the time. They would be patient, they would wait 'till the right moment. They gnashed their teeth and screamed and howled. Then disappeared as quickly as they had come.

"I saw them too," Clare said as she came around. " Some real nasty characters, aren't they?" Michael looked over at her and said. "Yes, they are real nasty characters." He slowly nodded his head. Then he said,

"You are not afraid, are you, it is good that you are not frightened." "No, I don't have a lot of fear, when I'm awake, nightmares come at night in my sleep. I dream of the time my family was killed in an explosion, I was helpless, or I'm helpless in the dream, not being able protect myself or the family.

"It's time to go." Michael said. She laid her head on the steering wheel and hoped she wouldn't throw up or pass out. So much had happened in the last day or so, and at times, she wondered if she was dreaming. She was dizzy from not eating all day, and she was very thirsty. She reached behind her seat where she kept a bag of snacks and a six pack of bottled water, she handed Michael a bottle of water and the snacks. The heat of the Florida sun pretty much was the proverbial 'pinch on the arm' that assured her she wasn't a participant in a horrible nightmare but rather a horrible reality.

They pulled onto the interstate and headed west to Marion. "We have to go to Patoaka to see Veronica first, said Michael. "Why do we have to go to Patoaka and who is Veronica?" "She is the woman whose mother is in danger." We go to Patoaka first, then Marion.

Chapter 15
Whippoorwill Lane

"Patoaka is fifty miles out of our way," she said. "Veronica is the daughter of Susan Ginsburg, who lives at Wedgewood Manor, she is the one we have been sent to help. You'll be safe at her home, they won't come onto her property while I'm there, even though you may see them through the barrier. You will need time to prepare, and you must rest a day or so."

Clare was exhausted, too exhausted to ask Michael all the questions welling up in her mind. She decided to drive on in silence. She knew she could not handle another crisis between now and the time they got to Patoaka. She longed for the cool spring air of upper New York.

She was not emotionally prepared to help anyone. "Strength in times of battle, times of battle, what am I thinking?!" Clare said to herself. "That's what this is, a battle, a horrible battle that somehow, I got roped into by this Michael sitting next to me, a battle that I have been chosen to fight alongside Mr. Mike here" she thought.

Michael turned to Clare, "yes Clare," he said softly, "this is a battle you are called on to help fight". "I'm way too tired to get into this Michael, you are a whole lot stronger than me, why can't you handle this yourself?" He was silent for a good ten minutes before he responded to Clare's question.

"I am bound by my Creator to do what I was created to do. I banish that which destroys innocent souls. I can only defend in times of battle when innocent souls choose to be defended from the evils that roam the world. "What about my husband and parents?" Clare said. "They didn't choose to be evil, they were the farthest thing from evil, my God, Gerry was a healer!" They didn't choose to die."

"No, they didn't choose to die, Michael said, "they were victims of a great evil that has escaped from the depths of hell, an evil that comes when too many people cooperate with evil, like a seed it grows and grows and causes a rift, it hides in the grave afflictions of mankind, in their bodies. Your husband had just banished a demon from a dying patient, that it had occupied for a long time, it was strong, and came back to destroy Gerry, for taking his patients' body *and* soul from it, the demon cannot take a soul as easily as it can destroy a human body.

Those demons can possess, manipulate, and torment humankind. They cannot take the soul of the faithful, but they can physically torment them. The good in those people, the faith they have in their Creator the mercy they receive from Him preserves their souls. What killed your parents and husband is one of those demons, it came to hurt you the only way it could. Because you and those like you pose a great threat to them.

By taking away all that you loved in this world. It came to punish you, make you suffer, for the gift you have and for all those you stole from them, all those healed by the gift you were given at birth.

A rift, a portal, is forming at Wedgewood Manor, where Veronica's mother lives. It began over a century ago. Should it open, Perditus will roam this world, and release upon mankind a suffering beyond all imagining, as it has done, since the beginning of mankind. It is my task to banish it back to the bowels of hell. That I can do. I cannot save a soul, only the choices humankind will make, will save them. If Susan receives your help and her daughters' forgiveness the portal will close back. The old woman is the last bit of human cooperation it needs to burst through. She is weak but grasps onto life, in the hope of being saved from an eternity of misery."

Clare knew. She had always known but never heard anyone articulate as well as Michael. She knew there were various levels of evil, she knew. Sadly, she realized that unlike her husband, she wasn't as willing to commit to the demands of the gift. She began to realize how self-centered she is, and how much she pitied herself and yes, how proud she allowed herself to become. She resolved to grow up. Bite the bullet. Move on and embrace the precious gifts that were bestowed upon her.

She was glad Michael sought her out. He was quite a guy. Odd but so special. Like her, only better, like Gerry, only stronger. She had no idea how many people in the world, were like him. Capable of so much good.

They turned off the interstate, and took the rural route west for another eight miles to Patoaka. They passed through the center of town, four roads branched off east, west, north and south, the town Courthouse stood in the center of the intersection. They took the route that went north and drove several miles, "turn at the next mailbox," Michael said. Clare followed the road until they came to a mailbox at the road that read "Whippoorwill Lane." They drove up the dirt road under a canopy of Live Oaks that dripped with Spanish Moss, bushes with lush lavender blooms lined a gravel driveway. Clare dodged an occasional pot hole as the driveway twisted around for three hundred yards or so. They pulled up to a pale-yellow stucco house with a Spanish roof. Two Magnolia trees with heavy scented white blossoms stood like sentinels on either side of the two-car parking lot. Spirea bushes and azaleas, in full bloom, brushed up against the sides of the house.

Two fig trees stood to the right of the front deck. In a fenced in area, near the house was a garden, tilled, ready to be planted. The soil had been turned over and boasted a rich loamy black soil, the product of years of cultivation. "I think I am going to like it here," Clare whispered to herself.

She had a sudden memory flashback of her childhood in Marion, before the fire, a time of joy, beauty and love. She choked back tears as she remembered her parents and the beautiful Greenhouse, the beautiful shrubs, trees and exotic flowers. So vivid was the flashback that her head filled with the fragrance of gardenias that grew profusely all around the greenhouse.

Clare had come a long way, she was tired, exhausted and weak. The place and all its beauty were so soothing to her. She stepped out of the truck and for the first time in several horrible days she felt safe. Veronica came out to greet them as they pulled up to the house.

She was tall, silvery white tendrils of hair peeked out beneath her sun hat. Her denim shirt and jeans were loose on her lanky figure. The sleeves were rolled up to her elbows.

She was tan and weathered, indicative of someone who spent all their time outdoors. She approached them without suspicion, as though she knew them. "May I help you?" Her clear blue eyes, set in an open inquisitive smiling face, looked right through them.

Michael stepped forward and stretched out his hand, "Veronica, my name is Michael" As their hands connected Veronica looked up at Michael in gratitude and relief. "Thank you for coming. I knew someone would come." She invited them in. She looked at Clare's haggard state, she sensed that Clare was at her home to rest.

"It is safe here, they can't come onto your property," Michael looked over at Veronica and smiled. "You are gifted *and* a favored one. If only all the gifted were as vigilant as you, the world would be less vulnerable to hellish destruction." For the first time since he and Clare left New York, Michael appeared serene.

Veronica rarely had people over and rarely interacted with her community or neighbors since her husband died. She had come to accept a life of some social isolation. Yet she was not by nature an introverted person. It was just that she couldn't block the psychic ability to read the people in her path. She knew that she was called to help them, that's what the 'gift' was all about, she never doubted that.

But sometimes it wore her down, and sometimes if someone was acutely under the influence of an evil presence it would affect her as well, which was physically and spiritually painful. To go to town, walk down the main street of shops, busy with people coming and going, proved to be so mentally cacophonous that it was all she could do to keep from running as fast as she could all the way home. But she managed to brace her psychic self, and as she walked among people she radiated peace, to all who passed by her.

She welcomed the isolation of her home and gardens after a long day in town, here she would recharge and the grace that flowed through her outweighed human loneliness. She was happy to have a guest especially two who were on the same spiritual plane.

Clare and Veronica became instant friends and together prepared a light dinner which Clare ate voraciously and without reserve. Michael sat quietly as the ladies chatted over dinner about their experiences with the 'gift'. Seeing that Clare was exhausted, Veronica invited her to stay the night, that she had a guest room at the top of the stairs.

Gratefully, Clare excused herself from the table and followed Veronica to the guest room. "You will find a nightgown and robe in the dresser by the bed. The room has a private bath and it has whatever you need for a bath or shower." Veronica said.

When she returned downstairs, Michael was in the back of the house, he stood on the back deck, and looked out towards the gardens and the setting sun. They spoke quietly about why he and Clare came to Florida. He confirmed her suspicions about the situation with Lyla, that she had not represented truthfully the full situation with Susan. Susan was too weak to correct her afflictions herself, and was under a constant barrage of spiritual warfare, she was alone in her spiritual fight, weak and unfocused, one moment angry and mean, the next minute she was remorseful and attempted to pray. If she died without forgiveness, her soul would be locked in the house until the end of time.

What he didn't tell Veronica, was that a horrible evil would be unleashed beyond the confines of

Wedgewood, an evil that must be dealt with before Susan died. Her sister Lyla, had become a life-threatening risk, a lightning rod, a catalyst to the evil in the house. He knew that Veronica was already aware of Lyla's problems, but she did not know that Lyla had become possessed with murderous and destructive tendencies, or that her sisters plotted against Susan. Clare and Veronica's work was cut out for them.

They did not know the full scope of the battle they were about to undertake, Michael was confident they would do what needed to be done at the right time. Veronica's sisters would be gone from the house in a few days, until then, Clare would sleep to regain her strength.

Veronica's house was free of any evil presence. After the girls went to bed, Michael sat downstairs in the dark of the living room. He stared out the window as though hypnotized by something he saw. He sat in silence, his legs stretched out in front of him, he was still dressed in the Bermuda shorts, tropical short sleeve shirt and sandals that Clare bought for him. His skin bore no signs of the pinkish skin of a fresh Florida tan on flesh exposed to sun after a long winter, rather his skin was as alabaster white as the day he introduced himself to Clare.

Only now as he sat gazing up into the night sky he exuded a slight glow all about him, even his black shoulder length hair was alight in a halo of soft light. Silent and unmoving, he remained fixed in this position until dawn.

Clare slept for twelve hours. The next few days and nights the two women became good friends, Veronica took Clare all about the eight acres. They delighted in the gardens and chatted about this plant and that plant. They shared their knowledge of horticulture and botany. They did not speak of their special gifts.

Michael seemed to disappear during the daylight hours. He said he needed to checkout a few things and would be back soon. Veronica was quick to refer him to Saint Nicholas Monastery just a few miles north of her place. "It's quite lovely Michael," she said, "you will love the gardens, the monks keep to themselves, but allow the public to walk about to enjoy the grounds."

Michael returned at dark, and passed up dinner because he said that he already had his evening meal in town. He went to the downstairs guest room until Clare and Veronica were in bed, and then he returned to the living room and sat in the dark, facing the window and there he remained until dawn, in a soft halo of light.

Chapter 16

The Cruise, *Southern Winds*

Lyla stole a check from her mother's checkbook, wrote it for fifteen thousand dollars and signed her mothers' name. It wasn't the first time she forged a check, it was just the first time she forged a check in the amount of fifteen thousand dollars. Lyla was quick to learn her mother's signature and was able to fool Susan and even her banker old Stan McCray, a good friend of the family. Anytime she had any banking business to tend to Susan always sought out Stan. Part of having Stan help her was that it was a nostalgic way to reconnect with Carl, through his friends.

Stan always took a few moments with her to reminisce about this and that and do you remember when stories. Carl was one of Stan's best friends. They had a unique connection, yes sir, he had an easy way, open and friendly. These days when Stan looked around the bank, he saw young men and women striving for the better bank positions, the teller supervisor position or the loan officer positions, and the elite senior banking positions. They strode around the bank like peacocks and princesses, yes sir, peacocks and princesses, all dressed up in their fancy suits that Stan could never afford when he was their age. They drove sporty new cars in flashy colors.

Like Carl, Stan was of the old school he bought second hand cars, and suits on sale. Not like the young 'executives' expensive designer suits, rather Stan chose off the rack run of the mill (but nice) work suits, after all they represented the public and Marion County Bank was a far cry from Wall Street, where everyone wore four hundred-dollar suits or, so he was told. He resented the younger generation and their garish ways.

Prior to his semi-retirement, Stan was a senior loan officer, his job description included writing loans for farmers such that they could finance major farm equipment, worth a minimum of a quarter million dollars. This was done by Jim Speed now. After thirty years, Stan met retirement with grace. He wanted to make sure the transition from himself as Senior Loan Officer to Jim went seamlessly.

He taught Jim Speed everything he knew. He was proud of that. After all, some employees who retired found ways to make it hard for the new employee to take their place, by telling them a lot of 'misinformation' or welcomed their successor with empty file cabinets, empty of all the important files. He often overheard them laugh and joke about it in the lunch room. "There goes another sucker!" They would say, about a new employee. But not Stan, he was a man of integrity.

Stan was the last of his generation, all the employees his age were retired except for him. They allowed him to stay on after his initial retirement at the information desk. So here he was, the last of his 'kind' that still clocked in at eight o'clock every morning, Monday through Friday. He still wore his nice suits, but instead of writing loans for customers, he greeted customers.

He liked the job, there were so many people he knew and not just the people his age, but also their children, now married with kids of their own. Everyone knew his name and he knew theirs. Sometimes a young cashier would approach Stan to verify a signature or customer, they didn't recognize, and he would look over and would say "Oh that's so and so' son, and then looked at the customer signature on a check and officiously give an okay nod to the teller.

He didn't know whether it was the man's handwriting or not, it just so happened that one day a young sweet teller didn't know who to go to and he just happened to look like he was important, so she asked him if this signature was valid or not. It helped that he glanced over at the person who just happened to be his former pastor and who never wrote bad checks.

After that, it became a kind of tradition at the Marion County Bank. "Stan knows everyone's handwriting, he can tell you whether it's a bad check or not," the head teller would say to new tellers. But Stan didn't know everyone's handwriting and he certainly didn't know that Lyla was about to cash a check for fifteen thousand dollars with her mothers' signature a blatant forgery.

Susan routinely checked her balance before she became bedridden. She was meticulous when it came to the bank accounts. She would look at her signature on checks written to cash, and although not remembering when she wrote these checks, or for what, she always accepted that it must have been for something important.

When her memory began to fail, she was alarmed at how much money had been spent in one month, but she knew she forgot things like who she wrote checks to, so she decided it was time to trust Lyla to keep the books. She was so afraid of not having enough money in the bank that she always maintained a balance of sixteen thousand dollars in her checking account. Today however, there was only one thousand dollars in the account because Lyla withdrew fifteen thousand dollars and deposited it in her own account.

Lyla looked at the perfectly forged signature on her mother's check and put it in her billfold. She drove to town and went to the Marion Travel Agency where she booked a Sailing/Fishing Cruise for six days for two. She dialed Marla on her cell phone and spoke to her for a few moments. They agreed to meet at Wedgewood in the mobile home adjacent to the Manor in one hour. Lyla then drove over to the library and at one of the public computers she pulled up a blank document and typed out a form that read:

April 15, 2017

I Susan Ginsburg of Wedgewood Manor, 4563 Palmetto Road, Marion, Florida hereby release Lyla Ginsburg of her responsibilities of elder care for me for a period of six days. In her place I agree to have Susan Mallory CNA, care for me.

Signed *Susan Ginsburg*

Signature Lyla Ginsburg

Lyla smiled at her handiwork, printed out two copies on the library printer, paid the librarian fifteen cents per copy and left the library with the documents in a manila envelope, tightly tucked under her arm.

The perfect plan for Susan's accidental death was underway. Lyla's heart beat fast in her bony little chest, and she walked stiff legged to her car, her thin lips in a tight grin. She bit her lip to keep herself from cheering out loud. The thought of her mother dead was sheer ecstasy.

Her eyes darted back and forth as she looked left and right. Sometimes she would wince at the screaming and laughter in her head, it was excruciatingly loud. In contrast to the lovable Pig Pen character in the Charlie Brown comic strip, whereby a visible cloud of dust hovered about him everywhere he went, an invisible legion of evil filth hovered around her, in and out of her, above her and below her, as she walked to her car.

She drove to the Manor to meet Marla. She knew that after a few days Susan would not be able to contact her or her sisters. Thanks to Lyla's elaborate lie, that she ran into Veronica at the Marion Orchid Show and she mentioned that she was going out of town. Her mother was resigned to Veronica's absence.

When Susan asked whether she left a phone number or address where she could be reached, Lyla lied again and said how thoughtless of Veronica to forget to leave a contact number where she could be reached. She lied again when she said she and Marla would be a phone call away. The truth however, was that she and Marla would be in the Bahamas, and with Cayla in Australia it would be a minimum of at least five days before anyone would get to the Manor in the event of an emergency.

Her mind raced with fool proof methods of murder. Lyla tingled with excitement. She could barely stand her bad self. This was the best idea she and Marla had ever concocted. Their mother's death would be because her non- existent nurse never showed up, and that her daughters were all out of town. The plan was perfect.

She would tell the authorities that she had arranged for a nurse to come in while they were gone and had the documents to show for it, referring to the false note she printed out at the library. "We trusted that our mother was in good hands," Lyla would tell the authorities. She would lie to them and say that she saw to it herself that Susan would be cared for by a trained CNA that she handpicked herself.

She drove up to the Mobile home, and gave a sideways glance to the Manor as she unlocked the door. Susan was not at her bedroom window today. On previous occasions Lyla saw her move from one window to another, always in her white nightgown. She confronted her mother about going up and down the stairs. "It's dangerous for you to go up and down the stairs mother," she said. "I would hate to come in and find you dead on the floor from a nasty fall." Susan always denied that she left her room.

About an hour later she heard the crunch of gravel as Marla drove up. Her thick shiny black hair framed her creamy white round freckled face adorned with a pair of three-hundred-dollar designer sun glasses. She got out of the Volvo that her ex-husband had purchased with funds from an eighty-thousand-dollar business loan that was to boost his custom auto repair business. Marla's second husband Bill Scott thought marrying into the Ginsburg family would raise him to new heights. Everyone in the community loved the Ginsburg family, and their reputation was stellar.

He didn't anticipate a wife with a lust for money, drugs, alcohol and sex. He went along with the life style, even participated in the swinger's parties that floated in drugs and booze. After too many nights and days in drunken stupors and frivolous spending, he knew it was a big mistake, the funds were to get the business going not pilfer away on things they didn't need, like cars and trips to Miami, Disney World or junkets to the Bahamas and the Bermuda Islands. Thanks to Marla's lust for shopping and spending money he went bankrupt and the business failed.

After the loan monies dried up, Marla told her parents how bad a husband he was and that he had a terrible addiction that she kept secret. Yes, she knew it was wrong, but she loved him. Her parents paid for her divorce, sympathetic suckers that they were. So, she got her divorce, her eye already on another man, with pockets full of money.

Marla got the car in the divorce which was the best she could do since her husband proved her addiction to drug and alcohol by way of records and receipts for three rehabs during their marriage. She didn't count on having any other fall out from her husband, so it came as a big surprise when the Courts garnished her wages because her signature was on the eighty-thousand-dollar business loan which required monthly payments, and which meant they were both responsible for the loan.

She had a job as a secretary with the local social services and once her wages were garnished, she realized it would be better to 'lose' her job and claim unemployment than to have her salary garnished. She had a way of pursing her lips when she thought she was pulling a fast one and getting away with it, and that is how she greeted the unemployment clerk, her lips pursed as he reviewed her case.

She lit a cigarette, inhaled deeply and exhaled slowly. This afforded her a bit of an 'I'm in control persona' as she nonchalantly approached the door to the Mobile home, the mobile home that was originally meant for Lyla, but when Marla got married Lyla offered it to her and her husband as a short-term wedding gift that was until they could get a place of their own. They never got a place of their own.

With Marla in the Mobile home, Lyla then had an excuse to live in the Manor house with her mother under the pretense that she would care for Susan, keep the house clean and care for the grounds. She kept a key to the Mobile home, just in case something happened, and she had to get inside, like today.

Lyla opened the door, "Quickly," Lyla said, "Mom could be watching, it's like she has eyes behind her head, she always knows what's going on here, hopefully she won't take the chance to walk down here and fall down again, I hate when she does that!" Lyla put a pot of coffee on and set out two cups and saucers on the small round table in the kitchenette along with a bottle of single malt Scotch whiskey. She poured the coffee and then put several jiggers of whiskey in each cup.

She set a brochure on the table with a picture of a Sloop sailboat. The brochure boasted a six-day sailing excursion that included fishing, and voluntary participation as part of the sailing crew, and when they got to Freeport, Grand Bahama, for three nights, they would go gambling in the famous Casinos and hang out during the day on the pure white beaches.

Marla read aloud,

"Join the F85 Sloop, Southern Winds" as working crew-guests for an exciting sailing experience from Fort Lauderdale to Freeport, Grand Bahamas and back. Must be totally honest and dependable, reasonable, flexible and be able to work and play well together. The luxurious 85-foot Sloop is designed for speed and style. Guests will love the spacious salon, dual helm amidships, galley and dining area.

You will also enjoy access to above lounge and sun lounge aft with swim platform that is also equipped for deep sea fishing. The spacious salon below has seating area port side with a large wrap around dinette to starboard. The galley is separate and forward with cabins for the professional crew.

Guest cabins are located between the master cabin and the salon and they feature queen berths, hanging lockers, storage and suite head compartments. She is powered by a Gummins turbo diesel engine and in addition to the full Sloop rigging, she boasts a five-ounce Gennaker sail designed to generate speed.

She sipped her spiked coffee, and continued to read through the brochure, she smiled and nodded her head. Finally, she looked up and said to Lyla, "in your dreams Lyla, it says we need five thousand dollars per person, and that doesn't include the gambling money in Freeport. We need at least a thousand extra for each of us to just walk into the Casino," Marla said sarcastically. "What do plan we do, rob a bank or something?"

Lyla said, "It is four thousand a piece for the cruise to the Bahamas and back, and we will have a thousand bucks a piece for gambling, and other fun stuff. I did not rob a bank, I did however rob a bank account," Lyla boasted, "I took money out of Mom's account. You know the one that has a sixteen-thousand-dollar balance because she's afraid she'll get overdrawn and have to pay a penalty fee? I happen to be a very good signature forger, she has no idea what her balance is and will never miss the bucks."

Lyla sat back with a smug look on her face, and sipped her coffee, "We have fifteen thousand in cash and sister we're going to have some fun," Lyla bragged. Marla and Lyla clinked their cups together and began to make plans for their departure. They had much to do.

Marla decided that they needed to go shopping and get the clothes and accessories for the trip. She wrote a list of things to take with them. They had two days to shop but Marla didn't want to waste any time and she planned to go to Orlando as soon as she left Lyla, even if she was a little tipsy. The thought of the upcoming shopping spree was exhilarating, and the thought of spending lots and lots of money was sheer intoxication.

She knew that Susan would be all alone once they left, and she will be dead when they get back from their sailing trip. It was a perfect plan. For the first time in their lives there would be no boundaries.

As they sat drinking and laughing, legions swarmed in and out of them, licking them and biting on their necks, wetting Lyla's and Marla's sensual appetites for some real fun on the sailing cruise. The outside of the mobile home became incased in a veritable dark grey cloud of slithering shadows that swarmed around and about it.

Later that night, the old Manor's creaks and moans woke Lyla with a start, the digital clock on the bedside table blinked three o'clock. She heard someone scream, once then twice. She got up to check on her mother and that's when she saw the woman in white walk down the hall and turn to go down the stairs.

She remembered when Veronica had mentioned that to her some years ago, how she had seen a woman walk down the hall in the early hours of the morning. Lyla thought perhaps that wasn't her Mom who peered out of the windows during the day, maybe it was this woman, especially since she was wearing that white gown. Maybe it wasn't Susan at all.

Susan was in her rocker, near the window when Lyla came in to the room. Lyla didn't turn on the light but rather walked into the room and listened. "Over here Lyla," Susan said. Lyla nearly jumped out of her skin. "Mom, you nearly scared me to death. I thought I heard someone scream," Lyla said in her most comforting voice. "You did," said Susan. Lyla stood for a moment wondering how to respond. "The woman in white was here and walked right down the hallway, used to be a bath there," Susan said.

"Did you see her?" Lyla said, "Of course I did, and you saw her too, I watched you look after her as she passed by your bedroom." "I always thought that was a bunch of crap, Veronica's spooky tales," Lyla said. "I thought so too," said Susan. "The Lady in white is the icing on the cake, there are others here that push me around, sometimes they try to push me out of my bed, I hate it when they do that. Remember when Veronica told us about the time someone tried to get into bed with her, and pulled down the sheet as though they were going climb in next to her? Well that is not all they do, sometimes they hurt me, bruise my arms and neck, sometimes they scratch me, once I thought someone bit me, the next morning I had bite marks on my leg.

Later Veronica told me that they got into her head and she could see them in her minds' eye, that's what she said, 'her minds' eye.' There were three people and they had their eyes closed and then they opened their eyes and looked right at her. "This is way too creepy for me," Lyla said. "I'm going to the kitchen and make us some tea, I'll be right back."

Susan continued to rock back and forth, she was wide awake, and pondered what had just happened. She saw the apparitions most nights now, they abused her and wearied her. Especially since they would wake her up and entertain her in their macabre way throughout the night with their screams, moans, cries, they paced back and forth, and continued to scream, moan and cry. Lately, the tone of their misery had changed to a more savage hellish sound that threatened mortal danger. This left her exhausted and tired most of the day.

Sometimes, she would be awakened by a painful pinch to her arm, or the woman in white stood at the foot of her bed and screamed down at her. She continued to endure the nights when she would be pushed out of the bed, or her bedding pulled off her, a dark unseen trespasser would get in bed with her.

On those nights the room got very cold and black, and the stench of death, on the frigid breath of the dark unseen trespasser, passed by her face, and it would softly laugh in her ear, "Soon, very soon, I'm coming for you," it would say. When it touched her, it would hurt her until she cried out, "dear God help me!" Usually that would end the torture for the time being.

Night after night now for several months Susan was awakened by one ghostly episode after another. She wasn't sleeping well, and her body bore the bruises on her arms and legs of the previous nights' activities. The sounds of the house became magnified. The creaks of the house became louder and louder, footsteps could be heard everywhere.

Voices came out of thin air and the infernal screams of the woman in white was incessant. She thought she would lose her mind. So, she would pick up her prayer beads in her shaky hands and hold them close to her chest, and tried to remember the prayers that she knew so many years ago, prayers that she discarded in her pride.

Lyla made a small pot of tea. She let it steep a few minutes, then set it on a tray, together with a small bowl of sweetener. As she reached up to get the tea cups she saw a reflection of someone in the kitchen window. It was behind her, in the kitchen, watched her as she looked back at it. She turned quickly around, and it was gone. "It's late and when one is tired stupid stuff happens," Lyla thought to herself. She took the tea tray upstairs, turned on a soft light in her mothers' room and set the tray down on the bedside table. "Let me help you get in bed mom," Lyla offered.

Susan got up from her rocker and let Lyla guide her back to her bed. "I know what you and Marla are doing," she said. Lyla nearly dropped the tea cup in her mother's lap. "What?" Lyla said looking as though she had swallowed a small bird. "You are going to get caught, and I'm not vouching for you anymore Lyla." Susan said in her dead serious voice. "You mean you know Marla and I are going on a six-day vacation, right?" "I know you stole fifteen thousand dollars from my account yesterday, I'm not senile Lyla," Susan said.

Lyla hit her mother hard on the side of her head with a closed fist, Susan fell back unconscious. "You say the darndest things! You feeble, old hag, see what you made me do? And then right in the middle of a conversation you just fall asleep," Lyla seethed. "Look what you made me do!" It wasn't the first time she attacked her mother, there were many times Lyla ended a conversation with a fast punch to Susan's jaw or a hard knock up side her head, as Susan confronted Lyla of something or other.

Susan never spoke of Lyla's late-night assaults on her, the next morning she would pretend that she fell out of bed and banged her head against the floor or some blunt object. It was enough that Lyla knew that her mother knew what she was up to. It didn't help that the bruises from the apparitions in the house were getting worse. Maybe she was senile, who would believe her if she told anyone about the abusive ghosts and her abusive Lyla, who would believe her. Especially since she already would excuse the bruises as falling out of bed. Indeed, who would believe her?

"She won't remember a thing" Lyla said to herself. She tucked her mother in and turned the light off and went back to her room, got into bed and fell asleep. She dreamt of sailing. The sun shone brightly, and the ocean breeze billowed the sails, as the sloop moved swiftly through the Caribbean Sea. At five o'clock in the morning Lyla woke, showered and dressed.

Usually Lyla would bring her mother a fresh cup of coffee, but today any thoughts about caring for Susan let alone saying goodbye to her was the furthest thing from her mind. She and Marla had much more important things to do, they would shop all day, pack, then head for Jacksonville, where they would stay overnight at the Marriott. Two blocks further from the motel was the

Palm Breeze Sailing Club and Harbor where the F85 Sloop was moored.

Chapter 17

Darkness Rises

The cold wet of her bed woke Susan the next morning. She winced when she felt the bruise along the side of her head. She sat up and waited until a wave of dizziness faded a bit. She was cold and wet and smelled of urine. She stepped onto the floor and held onto the edge of the bed as she made her way to the bathroom a short two feet from her bed.

The house was quiet. Susan sighed with relief. Most mornings it was the smell of fresh coffee that wafted up the stairs and a distant din of kitchen noise that woke her up. But today there was no clatter of dishes, pots and pans, or the hum of the dishwasher, there was no fresh coffee. Lyla went somewhere and didn't tell her.

That meant she would have to clean up after herself today. She glanced up at the clock on the bedside table, it read one o'clock. She had already slept half the day away. She tossed her soiled clothes into the laundry basket and turned on the shower. Usually she had about fifteen minutes before her legs began to give way and she would have to sit down.

She showered and got herself dressed. She generally chose her clothing by touch and color; her eyesight was too dim to make out details anymore. She reached for a pale blue cotton dress that hung over the back of a chair and slipped it over her head. She forgot that she wore the shift just the other day and that it was full of food stains all down the front of it. Stains that she couldn't see anymore.

    She couldn't see her toes, only the color and shape of her foot. It was too difficult to bend over and put her socks and shoes on, so she slipped into her red bedroom slippers that were always at the side of her bed. The effort to shower and dress brought on another dizzy spell, she sat on the edge of the bed and held onto the bannister until it passed. Sometimes the dizzy spells made her nauseous and she would throw up. Today her stomach was empty, she only gagged and perspired profusely. She couldn't remember when she ate last.

    Finally, she made her way to the vanity, she raised a brush to her short silver hair that had a mind of its own and with a shaky hand brushed her hair. She gazed at the blurred face in the mirror and noticed the bluish black mark blooming on the side of her face. She wondered if she fell out of bed again. She couldn't remember. She winced when she touched the bruise.

In the bathroom closet she had a little coffee pot, mug and a small can of coffee for those days when Lyla was out of town. She steadied herself against the sink and made coffee. She poured herself a cup and set it down on a small table by the window, she sat down in the rocker and pulled out her prayer beads and blessed herself. She tried to pray prayers that now, were very dim in her memory, all the while she gently rocked back and forth.

As she began her morning prayers even though it was afternoon now, it came to her and she remembered the episode with Lyla the night before. She wept for Lyla who hates her. She realized that she should have gotten help for Lyla a long time ago, she regretted the years of cover-ups for the many petty crimes she committed and when she wrote bad checks or stole money from people.

She realized she should have never paid for the attorney to defend her when she proved herself incompetent to teach and insubordinate to the school principal, which got her terminated from employment with the school system. She realized a lot of things that filled her with remorse. She was ashamed of her jealous heart towards her oldest daughter, Veronica. She regretted the times she got caught up in making fun of her in front of her sisters, she regretted how they held her up in mockery and how they seethed with uncontrollable anger and hatred towards her.

She wondered why she did these cruel things to her daughter. Susan wept. Her motherless behavior filled her with remorse. She prayed for forgiveness, she prayed for strength to do the right thing, she prayed and prayed until a blood curdling scream echoed through the house and startled her out of her prayerful reverie. She looked up and the woman in white hovered in front of her. Her face decayed and filled with rage.

She screamed again, pulled at her hair, and disappeared through the wall. There was a loud bang in the hallway. Susan got up to see what it was, the door to the enclosed stairway, that led to the fourth-floor attic swung open and banged against the wall, again and again. As Susan attempted to close the door, halfway up the stairway she saw a body that swayed back and forth, hung by the neck, its open eyes stared passed her, a hateful grimace upon its face. She quietly closed the door and locked it.

She put her prayer book and beads on the bedside table. She picked up her cane and slowly walked to the stairs. She only had one flight of stairs to go down. She gave up living on the third floor for some time now. She sat down on the stair lift attached to the wall and turned on the switch.

When she got to the ground floor she remembered she left her porta-chair on the upper floor. It would be difficult getting to the kitchen from the stair lift. She shuffled into the kitchen using the walls to help her and made herself a bowl of cereal. There was no milk in the refrigerator, so she ate the cereal dry. She couldn't find her medications. She looked in all the usual places, the kitchen table and the cupboard right of the stove.

The meds were misplaced, hopefully she would find them before too long. She made her way to the little sitting area where she liked to watch TV. As she sat down she saw two little girls in front of the fireplace. They turned and walked through the brick wall. She rarely if ever caught a glimpse of them in the daylight hours. But this afternoon she was greeted by the woman in white, the hanging man, and the little girls. She was becoming nervous and really needed to find those meds.

It was close to three o'clock when Susan made her way downstairs. She was very dizzy and still hungry even though she had the dry bowl of cereal. She sat on the sofa and waited for a dizzy spell to pass, she keeled over on her side and dozed off.

Chapter 18

The Trip Home

Cayla and her daughter Joyce embraced at the boarding gate. "You know Mom, it takes two days to get home from Sydney, so pace yourself and don't miss your flight out of Hong Kong ok?" Joyce said. "Don't worry dear, I'll be ok," Cayla said with a wince. Her arthritis was acting up and her arms, legs and hips were burning with pain. She hugged her daughter and smiled a weary smile. "I love you, take care of yourself," she said to her daughter. "We'll all be glad when this semester is over, see you in a few months dear." Cayla boarded the plane and found her seat. She was exhausted and hurt all over.

The trip to Queensland Australia was a bit more than Cayla bargained for. The two days to get there, the layover in Hong Kong and the Spartan accommodations her daughter had, made it all very uncomfortable for Cayla. Joyce was an exchange student at Queensland University. She was good at her studies and shared her parents' enthusiasm for competition. She was an honor student and a member of the women's rowing team that proudly boasted an undefeated season. She was the apple of her mothers' eye and her only daughter.

Unlike her daughter, Cayla was not a strong vibrant athletic woman. After decades of diet pills to cover the hunger, and pain of starvation, to overcome the discomfort of plastic surgeries, to calm the anxiety and fears of imagined imperfection, to mask the painful discomfort of deterioration of her bones and joints due to a lack of nutrients, to control the depression after years of obsessing over the endless pursuit of perfection, Cayla was exhausted.

She couldn't enjoy the busy itinerary that her daughter Joyce put together for them. The hiking, swimming, endless barbeques and evening gatherings of friends that came out to meet Joyce's mother overwhelmed her. She longed for a quiet day of pills.

Somewhere in the back of her mind she remembered something her mother told her, something she said about one of her high school sweet hearts. Ronnie had a crush on her from the time she was in the seventh grade. His father was a very successful farmer, on the Board of Commissioners, and a local philanthropist of sorts. Ronnie's father taught him how to drive tractors and he worked the land from the time he was twelve years old. By the time his father died his farm had grown into a major commercial agricultural operation.

Ronnie finished college with a BS in Agriculture and took over the farming business. They were childhood friends, until Cayla turned fourteen and noticed her reflection in the full-length mirror that hung on the back of her bedroom door, on the third floor of the Manor house. She fell in love with herself, and spent long hours gazing at her reflection. Every now and then she could swear something was smiling back at her in the mirror besides herself and she loved that too.

"You should have listened to Ronnie," her mother told her just before she left for Queensland. They never dated but Ronnie always loved her and stayed friends with her through high school. He always told her what she needed to hear not what she wanted to hear. He could be so annoying that way. But now, the things he said echoed more and more in her, so many years later.

At first, she didn't understand what her mother meant but lately little memories would come to mind. Memories like when Ronnie noticed when she lost a significant amount of weight in the tenth grade and said to her, "I liked you the way you were." Losing twenty pounds when you only weigh one hundred and twelve pounds to begin with did seem a bit over the edge now that she thought about it.

There was that time when she and her cool friends were sitting in the Sweet Shop across the street from school smoking cigarettes and weed, a cloud of smoke floating around their heads, Ronnie walked by nodded a greeting and said, "cloudy minds" and kept right on walking. She watched him walk right out the door, and off into his own world. There was that night after one of the football games when she and her cool friends attended an after-game party her parents didn't know about.

Some guys were handing out cans of beer to everyone walking in the door, she didn't notice that each can was already opened. She only remembered that Ronnie was looking down at her when she woke up the next day. He had gone out looking for her when she didn't come home that night. He went out as a favor to her mother, but also because her loved her and was concerned as much as anyone for her. He found her naked under a bush behind the football field. "I found your clothes over there" he said. "Here put them on and I'll drive you home, your folks have been out looking for you all night."

While he drove her home, Cayla remembered asking him what happened, and he said, "sometimes those parties can be risky business, you might want your mom to take you to the hospital and have yourself one of those female examinations." She was too embarrassed to go to the hospital. Cayla blushed at the memory of it all, especially since she did get pregnant and knew there was no way she could have a baby.

The thought of a baby was unimaginable back then. She got an abortion and never looked back until this very moment. She never told her mother either or her sisters. Only Ronnie knew, and he went with her to the clinic. "You don't have to do this you know," he said. "You could put the baby up for adoption, there are people who can help you get through this. When my brother Bobby came back from Viet Nam he said killing leaves a mark on you that never goes away. A mark that burns into your body, mind and soul, maybe you don't see it right away but eventually it comes."

She had the abortion anyway, thanked Ronnie for being such a good friend and went right back to school. It was after the abortion that she started ignoring Ronnie. Every time she saw him she pretended she didn't see him. He asked her to the Senior Prom and although she didn't have a date at the time she said she was already asked but thanks anyway. She did everything she could to dismiss him from her life.

But the memory she loved the best about Ronnie was when she had the plastic surgery on her nose. It was the summer before her senior year. That fall she came back to school with a pert little upturned nose. Everyone loved it. One-day Ronnie came up to her at the lockers between classes, and said. "You were beautiful the way you were." Like so many other times he just kept on walking.

Her mother was right, and she knew now what she meant. Why couldn't she see what she was doing to herself all those years ago? The bad dates, bad decisions, bad boyfriends, bad habits, all these things made her what she is today. She felt her body seize with anxiety and sadness. She couldn't control the past, she couldn't go back and correct surgery or the abortion which like a bad tattoo was one of those things that just won't go away no matter how hard you try to remove it, always in the back of her mind and always a pill pushed it further back. Her vanity owned her and there was no going back.

As soon as she settled into her seat she pulled out a bottle of painkillers and swallowed three pills with a swig from her water bottle. She felt very weak. The doctor told her before she left for Queensland that she needed to eat more, and that she has already damaged her heart from starving herself. She promised herself she would be good. The plane began to move and was soon in the air. Twenty minutes into the flight her pills were doing their magic and Cayla could feel the warm embrace of the painkiller and the burning in her joints subsided.

She fell asleep and dreamt of her mother sitting in her rocker reading a book. Suddenly, she felt as though an invisible swarm of mosquitoes were all around her and she swatted her arms and legs and face trying to rid herself of them. She looked to see if the mosquitoes got in through an open window in Susan's room. Then she said, "Cayla turn around." Cayla turned around and saw what looked to be several smoky shadows hover in the air, slowly making their way towards her. As they got closer she saw they weren't shadows but something that had very ugly faces and teeth. Cayla screamed as one took a bite out of her neck.

She woke up from her nightmare, her face drenched in sweat. Her chest was heaving as though she had been running several miles. Her hands shook uncontrollably. She swallowed hard and looked around only to see other passengers finishing up their meals. Coffee and tea were being served by the stewardesses. "Just a nightmare" she thought. She slowly got control over herself, her breathing slowed, and her hands stopped shaking. She pulled a Kleenex from her purse and wiped her face. Her tray was down, and her meal was in front of her. Apparently, dinner came while she was asleep.

She looked at the plane food and frowned. It was a pretty good meal for an international flight, and was well presented. Roast potatoes, grilled chicken and steamed broccoli still warm in its' plastic covered dish. She noticed that everyone had already eaten, their trays put up and many had gone to sleep while others read books, watched TV or worked on their computers. She had not eaten all day but had no appetite what with the diet pill she took earlier still in her system. She picked at the dinner and tried a few bites. That was all she could handle. She covered the dinner with its plastic cover. A stewardess came by handing out pillows to the passengers. Cayla handed her the uneaten dinner and took a pillow.

Still edgy from her nightmare and from the trip down memory lane she took several tranquilizers to calm her nerves and lay back on the pillow the stewardess gave her and tried to go back to sleep. "Just a nightmare" she said to herself as she sank back into a heavy drugged sleep. She dreamt she was dressing for a social event. She chose a silk blue gown with a gossamer wrap, a pair of matching heels.

She drew a bath and added scented oils and soaked in the tub. As she was drying herself off she caught a glimpse of herself in her full-length mirror. She gazed at her perfect body turning this way and that examining every curve and perfect muscle. Then she looked at herself full frontal and that was when legion made itself present to her. She saw in the mirror a reflection of herself with sheer smoky things crisscrossing in and out of her floating all around her. One slithered around the back of her neck, its eyes stared back at her in the mirror, it grinned hideously, stretched open its mouth and long fangs bit ever so quietly into her neck.

It didn't hurt, rather it gave her a sense of erotic satisfaction at the perfect body that reflected at her in the mirror. It suddenly didn't matter that black slithering things hideously ugly, swarmed all around her in fact she welcomed them. She was perfect in every way and that was all that mattered, and they made if feel so good.

Cayla drifted deep into a drugged sleep, her starved and weakened heart beat slower and slower until it simply stopped beating. It wasn't until four hours later into the flight that the stewardess discovered she had died. The stewards gently placed her body in a body bag and moved it into the cargo area of the plane. When the plane reached Hong Kong the airlines called her family and had her body placed in a wooden coffin, sealed it, then placed it in the cargo hold of a plane to Orlando, Florida where her husband was scheduled to pick it up.

Chapter 19

The F85 Sloop

Lyla woke up at five o'clock in the morning. She jumped out of bed and took a shower, dressed and went downstairs to the motel dining room. She poured two cups of coffee, put a few bagels on a paper plate with several packets of cream cheese and juggled it all back up to her room. "Wakey, wakey little sister it's time to sail," she sang. Marla peered out from her pillow and groaned. "What time is it?" "Time to make our way down to the pier and be counted," Lyla said. She checked the itinerary for the time they were to report to the Harbor Office. "We have to sign in at the Office in less than an hour, get moving Marla."

They pulled themselves together, checked out of the motel and drove the short two blocks to the Pier. "It's moored in slip number twenty-five," Marla said. They parked the car in the guests' long-term parking area and headed down the deck looking for their Sloop. "Holy cow," Lyla said. "There it is." It was more than either sister had imagined. The Sloop seemed longer than eighty-five feet, the mast was huge the sails were neatly tied.

They felt small as they stood next to it. It boasted a fiber glass hull painted blue and white, its' metal hardware and varnished deck reflected the early morning sunlight, the beautiful lounge area on the sun deck was most luxurious. It was beyond their wildest imaginings. They made their way to the Office and signed in. The room was abuzz with people that stood around in small groups sipping coffee and engaged in small talk and chit chat. Many guests were already tanned from previous sails, hair streaked with blonde highlights that only come from outdoor living.

A door opened, and several men and women entered the room dressed in navy blue matching polo shirts, white slacks, deck sneaks and navy-blue ball hats. This group Lyla guessed to be the crew. They lined up in single file and stood at ease with hands behind their backs. Then a man entered the room wearing a smart navy-blue blazer with a military style hat. Lyla was right to guess this was the Captain. He welcomed all the guests and read the roster to assure all were present.

Once all were accounted for the Captain explained their duties and paired each guest with a seasoned crew member. Lyla was paired with the team leader in charge of the sails. Joey, a tall, long muscled man, his skin weathered and tan with a sprinkling of gray in his otherwise unruly main of sun bleached brown hair greeted each guest on his team with a smile and a firm handshake.

Marla was paired up with the Chef in the galley. This wasn't exactly what Marla and Lyla had in mind, but at least they are on the sailboat heading out to sea. The crew helped everyone get settled and prepared the Sloop for sail. Once they were headed out to sea the Captain posted a schedule for deep sea fishing on the itinerary board in the main saloon down below.

Lyla loved fishing in fact she would do anything to get away from the Manor and go on a fishing trip, she looked forward to catching something big. Until then, she worked side by side with Joey who taught her the commands and methods of maintaining the sails. Lyla, along with three other guests, worked the sails the rest of the day. She felt the strain on her arms and back after all she was forty-eight years old. But she would not complain, everyone else was at least ten years younger than her and she was convinced she looked as good as the other shipmates and certainly as strong.

It was a beautiful day not a cloud in the sky and the winds were in their favor. The wind snapped and billowed the sails pulling them tight. The engine was turned off and the sloop was moving through the water at ten knots. It was exhilarating. Lyla wished it would never end.

At first Marla wasn't too keen on being a galley cook until she reported to Chef Charles, a tall fifty-year-old, handsome man, a little on the chubby side, with a twinkle in his eye and a quick smile. Marla was instantly in love. She was immediately put in charge of chopping the vegetables and washing the lettuces. She did such a good job Chef Charles allowed her to make the salad for the evening meal.

She kept looking over at the Chef as he worked on a French dessert. He was totally oblivious to her except when he came over to check on how she was doing. When she finally did catch his eye, he smiled at her and came over put his arm around her shoulders only to direct her to the dirty dishes which needed washing. He was a real charmer, but she didn't care in fact if he asked her to jump overboard she probably would.

The evening meal was wonderful. The entire crew and captain sat together and feasted on grilled steaks, fresh salad, stuffed mushrooms and potatoes, hot freshly made rolls and a delicious chocolate cheesecake smothered in a warm crème sauce. The wine and drinks flowed and soon music was playing, and some guests danced as others retired to the sun deck and laid out on the luxurious cushions drinking and enjoying the clear starry sky. The Captain retired to the cockpit and resumed his work. It was this time of the evening he chose to look away as the guests began to pair up for the night, often in the most indiscreet places.

As the guest crew members enjoyed after dinner drinks and sat out on the sun deck the hired crew manned the sailboat. The stars seemed so close that Lyla thought she could just reach up and grab one. She never wanted to see Wedgewood Manor ever again. She hoped the cruise would last forever. A brisk balmy breeze blew through the sails and the sloop cut through the choppy waters like a knife.

Lyla made her way to her cabin where she found Marla and the Chef rolling around in the queen size berth. She walked out in a huff and slammed the door behind her. She wandered down to the saloon, and sat at the bar where several guests sat sipping drinks. "How about a drink," a voice said behind her. She turned around and Joey stood holding a bottle of single malt scotch and two glasses. He poured the scotch, they clinked glasses, and suddenly her evening got much better.

Lyla didn't trust men. She had a kind of antagonism towards them. But she looked at Joey as her team leader and, so she tolerated the time he spent with her and sat, drank and eventually played a few hands of poker before she and Joey staggered back to her cabin and joined Marla and the Chef in the queen size berth.

A loud rap on the door woke them up the next morning. Lyla and Marla were naked and sprawled out on the bed like a couple of rag dolls. They woke with a start at the sound of the loud knock on the door. A deep voice announced, "breakfast is served in ten minutes." Hung over and with a dull headache, they staggered into the shower cleaned themselves up and prepared to head to the galley for breakfast that they both thought they would throw up.

As they entered the dining area a smiling Joey said a cheery "Good Morning ladies," winked as he handed them each a bloody Mary, and announced in his sexy deep voice, "We have a great day ahead of us!"

The next day they were in clear waters. The beauty of the Caribbean waters exhilarated Lyla and Marla. They couldn't wait to get to Freeport. The

Captain announced that the fishing chairs were ready for those who would like to try their hand at fishing. Lyla was the first one to strap in. The crew assisted in getting the deep-sea rods and reels baited and cast out for the guests. They handed Lyla the fishing rod, and strapped her into her chair. It wasn't long before she got a bite.

A magnificent sword fish took her bait, leaped out of the water one hundred yards off the stern, it splashed back into the ocean and the fight was on. The strength of the eight-foot swordfish was more than Lyla could handle. Rarely did a woman tackle the strength of fish this size. The assisting crew offered to take over for her, but she stubbornly refused even though her thin puny arms were strained to the max.

The tropical sun showed no mercy on her pale unweathered skin and it burned. Her already sore muscles from manning the sails the day before felt like they were tearing out of her arms, her back was freezing up in a nasty cramp. She was determined to show every man on board what she was made of, she was as good as any of them in and out of bed. Her determination was fed by the embarrassing moment when she woke up this morning and realized she had been laid and didn't remember any of it.

She fought the fish with angry pride fed by the nasty little shadow that whispered in her ear ways to get back at Joey. The fish was strong and was not tiring at all. Finally, one of the crew members offered to take over so she could get a little rest. Sunburned, and in agony from the pulled muscles in her arms and back she relented. But not without screaming rude remarks at the crew member who relieved her of the rod and took over fighting the swordfish.

The struggle to pull in the Sword Fish left her with searing pain throughout her body. She stumbled down below where she collapsed onto her luxurious queen size berth. Marla came in and put lotion on her sunburn and gave her several pain killers to ease her burned skin. "You idiot! That fish could have wrenched your arms out!" Gotta be a freakin' show off! What were you thinking, why do you think we have a crew?" Marla scolded.

"I thought I could pull it in" Lyla said proudly. "Well you made an ass of yourself if you ask me," Marla shot back. "The last thing we need is for the Captain to put you off the boat for crazy behavior, and you know what I'm talking about!" Marla didn't have to remind Lyla of the time she was thrown out of a bar because she got drunk and picked a fight with the bar tender, throwing glasses at him and calling him every expletive in the book.

Lyla slept for the remainder of the day. She woke just as the sun was setting. She could smell the delicious meal that wafted in from the galley. She tried to sit up but was completely immobilized with pain. She couldn't move, every muscle in her body screamed and burned. She was red as a beet, nauseas and swollen. With no sun exposure prior to the cruise and the long hours above board without any protection from the sun, she managed to get sun poisoning,

She was angry at herself and humiliated. She didn't think she could face the deck crew when she made an ass of herself trying to bring in the swordfish. "I'll get them" she said to herself. "They'll be sorry for laughing at me behind my back," Lyla seethed. But mostly, she was angry at Joey for using her the night before. Nobody gets away with that.

Marla came below to check on her sister. "How are you feeling Lyla?" Marla asked. "How do you think I feel? I'm not able to move," Lyla said. "The Captain asked if you would like dinner down here since you're hurting. I told him you were in a lot of pain," Marla said.

Lyla looked up at Marla and said, "Only if you come down too and eat with me. Otherwise, I need a handful of those pain killers, I didn't pay thousands of dollars to eat alone down here in the bunk area."

Marla sighed and said, "I would really like to eat in the dining room Lyla, so let me help you get cleaned up ok?" "Alright," Lyla said, she winced at the thought of moving an inch. Marla helped Lyla shower and dress. She gave her a few pain killers, "here, this will get you through the night, and you should feel better in the morning, ok?"

Marla and Lyla came up and joined the crew and guests in the dining room. The murmur of voices drew silent as all eyes were now on Lyla, as she entered the saloon and sat down at the table. Looks of sympathy and concern spread over the faces of guests, as they winced at Lyla's swollen red face. Several crew members looked back and forth at each other and stifled a grin. "Quite a fight the swordfish put up this afternoon. You put up a good fight too. We got a picture of the fish, you should have a copy since you were the one that baited it." The Captain said. Lyla smiled weakly and thanked the Captain for his offer.

The painkillers were kicking in and Lyla felt slow and dull, certainly relieved at the lack of pain from the pulled muscles. Marla sat next to the Captain and was fully engaged in flirting with him, Chef Charles who sat on her other side and Joey who sat across from her. Lyla looked around and everyone was talking to each other. No one was talked to her. She ate in silence and got up when she finished her meal, grabbed the closest bottle of wine on the table and went on deck. No one noticed.

The ocean was kicking up a bit, salt spray misted the deck. Lyla didn't care. She stared out at the black sea, and drank straight out of the bottle of wine. She thought of her mother for the first time since she left the Manor, and wondered if she was dead yet. "If she is still alive when I get back, I will kill her myself," Lyla thought bitterly.

She was stretched out on the sun deck lounge near the bow of the boat, in a drunken and drugged induced stupor. She noticed what appeared to be snakes that slithered along the guard rail. Then they floated towards her, their eyes stared into her eyes, and they grinned at her. Legion gently settled on her shoulder and she welcomed them. They slid in and out of her, and her heart filled with hatred, the kind of hatred that exhilarates the senses, the kind that kills with calculated perfection.

Marla woke the next morning sprawled out naked, she smelled of sex and booze. Lyla lay flopped over the foot of the bed fully clothed. Sometime during the night two crew men found her passed out on the sun lounge and carried her back to her cabin. A loud bang on the door of the cabin announced their arrival at Freeport. Crew and guests were already dressed on deck bringing the sloop around to dock.

The two sisters hurriedly dressed for the day. Lyla winced in pain, swallowed a handful of painkillers then joined the rest of the crew and guests on the tour bus. They stopped for lunch at the Freeport Palm Restaurant that overlooked the ocean and ate lobster freshly caught and washed it down with vodka martinis. Lyla was feeling no pain. After a few more hours of shopping and sight-seeing they headed back to the sloop to change for an evening of glamour at the Casino.

Marla showered and changed into a red sequined dress a size too tight and an inch too short. She slipped on three-inch sandal heels and pulled her hair up into a ball of curls. Lyla sat on the bed too doped up to manage a shower. In addition, she had no fancy dress to wear to the Casino. "You go Marla, I'm want to stay here, I think I need to take it easy tonight," She said. Marla stood admiring her low-cut dress making sure just enough cleavage showed to encourage a prospective hook up. "Okay, she said. She kissed her sister on the forehead and bounced out of the room.

Lyla sat on her bed stoned. She was very angry and blamed Joey for all her pain. She seethed with resentment. The way she was seduced the other night became a recurring obsession in her mind, she was determined Joey would pay. She opened her suitcase and pulled out a leather sheath that held what some might call a hunters' knife. She always carried it in her backpack. She was glad she brought it on the cruise. Maybe force of habit, but now she knew she would use it. She waited until dark.

Once the guests left for the casino, the professional crew gathered in the saloon eager to start their first hand of poker. The clink of glasses, and laughter of the men echoed topside to the sun lounge, where Lyla hid herself. She untied the Gennaker sail and let it flap back and forth in the wind. Since it was Joey's responsibility to maintain the sails she hoped he would come topside to fix it.

Lyla lay hidden for an hour before Joey came topside to retie the flapping sail. As he reached up to secure the lines Lyla slipped out from behind one of the lounge couches and stabbed him in the back three times in quick succession, piercing the backside of his heart and lungs. Before he could turn around she pushed him off the sloop. He hit the water with barely a splash.

She left the sloop without being seen, and hid in the back of the empty tour bus that would head out to the Casino at midnight to pick up the guests. The driver pulled up to the Casino and went in to pick up the guests. Lyla slipped out after him and waited until everyone started boarding before she came out from behind some lovely blooming oleander and slipped into line.

It went off without a hitch no one suspected anything. Lyla felt great. It was her duty to rid the world of crappy people like Joey. It was a wonderful feeling to hurt people. She remembered how it made her feel when she would slap Susan around. Always, she knew she was doing the right thing, because it made her feel so good. She sat back in her seat with a dreamy look on her face, a swarm of shadows surrounded her, in and out of her, and intoxicated her with a heady exhilaration that can only come from the kill.

Chapter 20

Storm Warning

When the bus pulled into the Harbor there were half a dozen police cars, blinking lights of the emergency vehicle lit up the parking lot. Marla did not see Lyla until the guests started to get off the bus. Lyla worked her way up the aisle until she was just behind her sister and said, "Don't turn around, I'm here and I have been with you the whole time at the Casino, okay?" Marla nodded in agreement.

One of Joey's crew mates had gone topside to see what was holding him up, he wanted to know if Joey was going to play another had of poker. He found him, face down, his corpse floated and bobbed against the side of the Sloop.

The police had arrived sometime before the bus returned from the Casino. When the bus arrived, the police told everyone to remain on the bus and they loaded up the rest of the crew and Captain, and escorted the bus to the Police Station. They were convinced someone from the Southern Winds murdered Joey.

They had already searched the vessel before the bus arrived but found no murder weapon. The police had no intention of letting the guests and crew get away.

Some hours later, having found no reason to keep the bus load of people, who were by this time exhausted and frightened, many indignant at being suspected of a murder, the police reluctantly let everyone go, still, there was no weapon, and everyone had alibis, and it appeared that there were no suspects among the crew and guests.

The police sent the bus and everyone on it back to the Harbor. Joey's next of kin were notified and his body was bagged and set to fly back to Miami the next day. By the time the authorities released everyone, it was close to four o'clock in the morning.

Once all were aboard, the Captain announced that there would be a delay in the next days' departure, due to the late night at the police station, and that they were waiting for another First Mate to arrive to take Joey's place. They were also asked to remain in their rooms until at least ten o'clock in the morning, that a brunch would be served at that time.

It was a very disturbing twist to what was otherwise a great vacation for everyone. Suspicion and fear drifted through the sloop, the guests kept to their rooms, doors locked. The crew whispered among themselves as to who had it in for Joey.

Marla didn't speak to Lyla for a long time. She was quick to figured it out. It wasn't the first time a death occurred when Lyla was around. Somehow, she managed to get away with it. To even suggest to her sister that she was not at the Casino all night would be a big mistake, and she sensed her own life might be at stake if she provoked her. Besides she didn't know if the rooms were bugged.

In a situation like this you just never know. "I'm taking a shower," Lyla said finally. When Lyla had gone into the shower Marla jumped off the bed and began foraging through Lyla's clothes for her knife. She knew she must have hidden it on her person as all the rooms were searched. "You won't find it there Marla, you don't think I'm that stupid, do you?" Lyla whispered as she came out of the bath a towel wrapped around her body.

"Silly girl, it's where I always keep it when I hunt," she said as she opened her towel and around her waist was a thick leather belt that held her hunting knife. "In times like these, some things a girl never takes off." Marla was chilled to the bone. Lyla walked up to her sister and whispered in her ear, "I would never hurt you sister, you know that, don't you?" Marla considered her sisters' eyes and said in a most childish voice "yes."

Morning brought a brisk wind from the south east, the skies were filled with grey clouds and choppy waters bumped up against the side of the Sloop. Lyla went topside to the sun lounge, to drink her morning coffee, despite what the Captain ordered. She looked around at the other vessels ported in the Harbor, the area was abuzz vessels were being prepared for departure, many were already out to sea in the distance. She wondered if it was because of the 'murder.' She finished her coffee and headed to the galley for the brunch. Guests and crew were already seated, a soft murmur filled the dining area, many ate and spoke in whispered tones, others remained silent.

Once everyone was seated the Captain came out and announced, "We will be pulling out within the hour due to a storm heading this way. Many vessels have already left Grand Bahama, to outrun the storm, and that is what we intend to do as well. Sailing the Sloop will get rough, and only the most able of guests should consider sailing alongside the crew. The severity of the storm will depend on who will be topside, for your own safety, you must comply with my orders."

He ended by saying that he was fully confident that they would outrun the storm and return to port in

Miami Florida, safe and sound. With that, he wished everyone a good day. The adventurous guests were charged with excitement, and looked forward to the challenge of sailing through a storm. Lyla was glad a storm was coming, it proved to be a distraction from Joeys' death.

They pulled out of the port around noon, the skies were beginning to show purple clouds in the distance. The Southern Winds was among the last of the flotilla to leave the Freeport Harbor. The wind kicked up and waves rolled in higher and higher, which added to the excitement of the cruise. Everyone was on deck, the professional crew, gave orders to the guest crew to secure everything that needed to be tied down.

The Flotilla sailed together for several hours before they drifted apart, and sailed their separate ways, the vessels soon became small dots in the distance. When the rains came, they came fast and sudden, the ocean rose up and the sailboat lunged into a huge wave. The storm was near. "All guests please return to your cabins," said the Captain over the bull horn.

The rains pelting the decks and the sails became taut with wind. The pilot's knuckles were white as he struggled to control the steering wheel. Soon torrential rains were so heavy the bow of the sloop was invisible. "All guests below!" shouted the Captain, his face paled as he stared straight ahead, his greatest fear had been realized. Although the storm that moved south east was still behind them a Squall came out of nowhere and headed straight for the sloop.

He shouted for the main sail to come down and to secure the boon. Marla ran back on deck to get Lyla. The rain was so heavy she couldn't see her hand in front of her face, let alone her sister. Meanwhile, Lyla was having the time of her life and refused to go below.

She worked alongside the new first mate on the sails, a huge wind caught the boon and swung it around to where Lyla was standing. There was the sound of a bat hitting a watermelon, and in the chaos and blinding rain no one noticed that Lyla's body slipped over the edge of the sloop, into the huge waves, A huge wave hit the bow of the sloop and unbeknownst to anyone, smashed into Marla, knocked her off her feet, rolled her off the edge of the sloop and into the churning waters, both sisters washed overboard.

The winds screamed all around the vessel as it glided up one huge wave after another until finally the mast cracked and broke in two. The weight of the mast turned the sloop far left, at the same time it got hit by a fifty-foot wave flipping the sloop upside down. The squall tore apart the Southern Winds. It was a miracle that only two people were lost in the storm.

Chapter 21

Brimstone at Wedgewood Manor

Clare rose early and decided to walk through Veronica's gardens, she sipped a cup of coffee as she strolled through a long row of Floribunda roses that dovetailed into a six-foot-high tangle of overgrown azaleas. The colors were breathtaking.

She strolled through the azaleas, and then through a grove of fruit trees, large yellow lemons hung at arms-length, and mango trees with their branches bowed at the weight of its fruit, lined the walkway. The trees brought back memories of her childhood. She loved to pick the fruits and eat them right off the branches. It was the perfect place to sit and eat the fruit. She remembered her parents' home, not far from here, and it brought back a flood of old memories. Even so, she longed to be back home at the Bristol Arboretum. It had barely been a week since she left New York, yet it seemed like an eternity.

She wondered when Michael would let her know what he wanted her to do, or who she was to help. She had her strength back and she felt good, notwithstanding the foreboding sense of things to come. She was well rested and recovered from the horrific episodes of the past few days. She knew there was more to Michael than he was letting on. "He has special gifts," she thought to herself, as she rubbed her arm, the one that got broke. "Special gifts indeed," more than Clare could have imagined. She thought perhaps he was from the far northeast, perhaps a fisherman off Nova Scotia, or someplace like that, considering the clothes he wore when she first met him.

She continued her walk through a row of multicolored day lilies. Another flash of childhood memory caught her by surprise, "Spider lilies, spider lilies mommy!" she exclaimed as she tugged on her mother's arm. She was overcome with grief, tears filled her eyes. "Spider lilies," Clare said to herself.

She would have collapsed in grief, and fallen to her knees and wept were it not for Michael. "Hello Clare," Michael said. "Good morning Mike," Clare said as she wiped her eyes and snapped out of her mournful reverie. "Didn't see you standing there."

"Today we go to Marion," he said. Clare was about to ask what she was supposed to do when they get there, but Michael put his hand up and said, "you'll know when you get there." He turned and walked back to the house. Clare watched him as he walked away. "Such an interesting man, his skin still an alabaster white, with a translucent quality, with no sign of the Florida sun on his skin. Maybe he used a lot of sunscreen," she thought sarcastically.

She went back to the house entered through the kitchen, Veronica sat at the table, she looked up and smiled at Clare "Good Morning! How about a refill?" "I can get it," Clare said, and freshened up her lukewarm coffee. She sat across the table from Veronica and watched the thin wisp of steam curl above her cup. "Today we are going to the Manor," Clare said.

Veronica stared into her coffee, "Mother blackballed me from the Manor you know. The last time I spoke to her she said stay away, that she didn't want to see me. Yet a few days ago I felt an urgency to visit her." Veronica's eyes filled with tears. "It's hard to go over there, I had to emotionally separate myself from my sisters and mother. It's so uncomfortable and tense, sometimes I got physically ill when I walked in the door. Those things, apparitions or ghosts that float around in that house are horrible, I don't know how they can live there."

"Lyla is not at the Manor," said Michael who appeared out of nowhere. "Neither is Cayla or Marla, your mother is alone, and her health is failing, she tried to contact you, but your sister prevented it. We should go soon, or the evil you sense there will consume her."

Veronica believed the evil at the Manor was the root cause of all afflictions and sufferings her mother and sisters had over the years. She knew this, but never thought anyone would confirm the existence of the evil in the house, or the apparitions, the trapped entities that wander the place. Her sisters always treated her as though she was a moron.

It was eight o'clock in the morning when they got on the road. Veronica led the way, Clare and Michael followed behind in the truck. They drove towards the town of Marion, again Clare's memories flashed through her mind, the happy family times, the beautiful Botanical Gardens her parents built, the love her parents gave so generously. Finally, they drove through the town of Marion, then south for ten miles.

They came to a sign at the edge of the road, Wedgewood Manor Circa 1802. A long driveway brought them around to the side of the Manor. There were no cars in the driveway and it appeared no one was home as they pulled in and parked. The house was in need of a paint job, the grounds boasted mature gardens that were slightly overgrown, and need of tending. Several broken clay pots lay strewn about a wooden table on the weedy brick patio. The plants and herbs that lined the patio were wilted and dying from lack of water.

The door to the sitting room was locked. Veronica looked through the glass portion of the door but didn't see her mother. "She must be upstairs," said Veronica. Michael put his hand on the door knob and the door opened. "Oh!" said Veronica "I guess it was stuck!" They entered the house through the sitting room.

The room had a musty urine smell. Susan was nowhere to be found. They checked the kitchen then headed up the stairs, the stair lift was at the head of the stairs which meant she most assuredly was up there somewhere. Susan sat in her rocker, her eyes closed, her face tilted up as though she had been looking out the window. Her face was pale gray. Her mouth hung open and her lips were dried and cracked. Her rosary was wrapped around her right hand and her hand was up against her chest. Her left hand tightly gripped the arm of the rocker. Her breathing was shallow. She opened her eyes when she heard Veronica call her name. Susan tried to speak, "Go away!" she rasped. "Get out while you can, they are coming for me. You can't stop them! They are going to kill me, they will take you too. They are way too strong for us now."

Veronica quickly went to the bathroom and filled a cup with water and held it up to Susan's lips. "Shh, mom, hang in there," Veronica whispered to her. Susan sipped the water eagerly, her feeble body trembled as she took small gulps of water, some spilled down the side of her mouth. "Where is Lyla and Marla?" Veronica asked. "Why didn't someone call me, I would have come over to stay with you while they were gone," Veronica said. Her mother raised her hand and waved her question away, "It's too late for why's and where fore's," she said. "Death is coming for me," Susan said.

Veronica asked her when was the last time she ate and when was the last time she took her meds. Susan couldn't remember when she ate last and was sure the meds were downstairs somewhere. She told Veronica that Lyla always left several plates of meals, and bottled water for her when she went away. But she couldn't find anything when she went down to the kitchen.

While Veronica tended to her mother upstairs, she sent Clare and Michael downstairs to find Susan's meds and to fix something to eat. The meds were found in the garbage can, next to the refrigerator, all four bottles.

Clare pulled a roast from the freezer and defrosted it. She found a basket of potatoes, peeled enough for dinner, and made a salad from greens in the garden. Before long the roast sent an aroma through the house and up to the second-floor bedroom.

Veronica got in the shower with her mother and soaped her up and washed her hair. She had bruises, scratches and bite marks on her face, neck and arms. She changed the bed and cleaned her room. She helped her into some clean clothes and tucked her into her bed of fresh linens. Susan looked up at her oldest daughter and took her hand. "I have so much to say to you, Veronica. I've made so many mistakes, for years I've been terribly jealous of you, I just can't seem to help myself," she said. Some days I think of you, and I know you are my best daughter, but when your sisters are around it's as though some kind of hysteria comes into me, and it makes me feel good to think badly of you, God help me Veronica, I'm so sorry, can you ever find it in your heart to forgive me, I'm such a wretch."

Susan cried and cried, she covered her face with her hands. Veronica sat down on the bed next to her mother, and embraced her in both her arms, and they held each other, and gently rocked back and forth. Finally,

Veronica asked, "Where is everyone?" Susan took a deep breath and told her how Lyla stole money out of her account, as much as ten thousand dollars.

She told Veronica how Lyla hit her and sometimes knocked her out. She told her how she had been left for days at a time, that she knew Lyla and Marla hoped she would die while they were gone. Cayla was always so busy with her husband and daughter, that she hardly ever came to visit anymore. She knew Cayla was in Australia, and was supposed to be home in a few days.

She told Veronica about the fishing trip that Marla and Lyla planned. She didn't know where they went. She told Veronica that "Lyla always said that you didn't want to come here, and that you always had excuses as to why you never came by anymore."

She told Veronica about the ghosts, how she could see them, and how they were more and more abusive, and that's who gave her the bites and scratches on her arms. "They are waiting for me to die, they plan to keep me here, in this hellish house," Susan said, as she grasped Veronica's wrist tightly. "Perditus is coming for you, that's what the lady in white screamed at me," Susan said in a trembling voice.

Veronica looked down at her mother, and acknowledged the seriousness of what she said. She shrouded the fear that gripped her heart. "I'm going to get you something to eat, it smells like Clare has lunch ready." Veronica kissed her mother on the forehead, and headed downstairs.

It was much worse than Veronica thought. She wondered how much of what her mother said was just senility and fear. So far, she hadn't noticed any strange noises or goings on since their arrival. The house was very quiet.

She wondered if Clare had noticed anything. Of course, her sisters weren't here, and she always felt evil when they were around. Maybe it was just bad karma between her and her sisters after all. Veronica gave Susan her meds and assisted her mother with the meal Clare made for them. Susan ate a few bites but was too tired and weak to eat anymore and began to doze. "Be careful Veronica, the ghosts are very mean these days," Susan said, as she drifted off to sleep.

As her mother slept, Veronica examined her arms and legs. She was appalled at the abuse her mother had endured. Scratches, old and new ones, bruises, purple, blue, green, she was abused daily from the look of her injuries. But it was the bites on her legs that puzzled Veronica. She couldn't imagine Lyla biting their mother. The bite marks didn't look human.

She covered her mother, and got up to look at the walls, she had noticed earlier, scratches on the walls, and blood splatter, and the inhuman hand prints that led to the ceiling as though someone climbed the walls, she followed the hand prints up the wall and over the ceiling. Whoever made the handprints apparently could crawl on the ceiling.

Chapter 22

Michael

While the women tended to Susan, Michael walked the grounds and circled the house. The demons were on best behavior, he mused to himself. Old enemies that he had banished many times before. There was no time in Michaels world, only space. He had been in this space before, he should have cleansed the entire place as he had done in the east. But, there was always that chance that the land would not recover. He mused at the many deserts in this world. This world, so fragile, with its trees and plants, flowers and the living things, the birds and woods creatures, yes, they would perish in the cleansing fires.

The cleansings and banishments are not as easy as they used to be, the Wonderworkers, so few these days. Not like in the days of old, when they and his armies worked together to banish evil minions. But he found Clare and Veronica, there are others too, in far off places. They would do, they would secure the redemption of the old woman, that's what their task is.

While his orders were ever present in his mind, he wondered why the Creator chose humankind to favor. There is no answer, not for Michael, there is only his orders and he was eternally obedient. Once again, he must cleanse this place, and leave it intact, to be lived in again and again until misfortune presents itself to the inhabitants. Perhaps, not this space. Perhaps it will be inhabited by a Wonderworker. They were so few left. It was not for him to be concerned.

He had confidence in Clare, she could do it, he knew her as a child, he watched her grow, watched her heal, banish evil from others. She had encountered Perditus before and would not back down. His gaze settled on the house, he saw what the women could not see, not yet anyway.

He had his orders. Orders given so many millennia ago. He never judged mankind (a favorite prey of evil), for their weaknesses, how they succumb to evil, the choices that led to the loss of their souls, one at a time. Evil took it's time, it liked time, it understood time, it did whatever it took to accumulate in the souls and bodies of men.

He saw through the hundreds year old Manor, the evil within, indeed he likened it to a whited sepulcher filled with filth and decay. The Manor, once again, had become a window, that demons and all manner of wraiths peered through, that roiled over themselves pushing and howling to be released, a window to the depths of hell. He saw what the residents referred to as apparitions and ghosts of men from past generations. An ancient 'prank' of sorts, where by the creatures would take on the likeness of men long dead, a prank indeed, to entice and possess the living, and turn them into instruments of destruction, that turn each other and the whole of creation, into a place of hate.

He didn't question his orders. Susan could be set free of her afflictions, yes, Clare and Veronica, the instruments of her redemption. The Wonderworker Clare gifted by the Father of Lights, the Creator, would push back the minions. Perditus would be left to him.

Susan's soul, stood in the balance, one more soul damned to hell would shift the balance of good over evil, the invasion of this space would warrant a great cleansing before Perditus and his minions could be pushed back. There would be uncontrolled death and destruction. It was never a catastrophic event that unleashed evil over the centuries but rather an accumulation of evil that afflicted mankind, whole civilizations comprised of thousands of souls won over one soul at a time until the entire age mired in evil succumbed to destruction through wars and plagues and finally total annihilation, mankind turned back to the dust of the earth. He had seen it so before in other places.

Michael had one opportunity to banish Perditus and his army, back through the portal in the Manor. Susan was dying. They would fight for her soul. It was up to Veronica to forgive her mother, and her mother to ask for forgiveness. It would be up to Clare to banish whatever legion had hold on the old woman, healing her of all her afflictions especially her betrayal towards Veronica.

Then he would do what he had done so many times over the millennia and banish Perditus, the foul one, back to hell. He had his orders.

When Susan fell asleep Veronica joined Clare in the first floor sitting room. Michael appeared at the kitchen door, "We have to get Susan out of the house," he said. "She just went to sleep, and she may be too weak to move just yet," said Veronica. "They are coming for her," Michael said. Clare agreed with Michael, she remembered the horrible episodes on the trip to Florida. "If Michael says we leave, we do it without question." Just then a huge boom sounded throughout the Manor house. A screech, like metal tearing filled the house.

The house groaned, and the air bent in the room. "Uh-oh," said Clare. The interior of the house faded. The walls, furniture and the stairway slowly disappeared. What was once a furnished room becoming busy with shadows that skittered behind faded walls, that were now a transparent barrier that separated them from an eerie life force.

Clare suddenly felt as though she was in a fish bowl, and she was the fish, eyes looked in at her at every angle. Shadows became clearly defined bodies, limbs, angry faces, and eyes. They laid clawed hands against the barrier, and tested it, pushed against it.

The walls of the house gave way to a second dimension, visible through the flexible see thru barrier, that revealed the Manor's demons disguised as former residents, and evil entities, many that Clare recognized, that she banished from her customers over the years.

But there were others too, she had never seen before, that howled and snapped their horrific jaws, that bit at the air, that stared back at them with hateful eyes. The three-story house, once a beautiful historic Manor house, had transformed into a House of Horrors, a labyrinth of horror that deceptively hid the interior of the house from them to keep them lost and confused, to keep them away from Susan and a hellish death.

Clare knew instinctively that the house was still here, she collected her energy and breathed deeply several times, a warmth ignited within her, and pulsed through her veins, it radiated through her skin, a halo of light bloomed about her, and surrounded her.

The interior of the house became visible, and the evil wraiths shrunk from Clare, amidst screams and howls. The din of noise and intensity of evil was great and took everything Clare had to concentrate and remain focused, as she and Veronica made their way up the stairs towards the old woman's room. She dared not give way to distraction, with the aid of the divine light she did not see the horrid creatures, but she could hear them, their whispers weighed heavy in her mind, she felt them crawling around in her head.

At the top of the stairs the lady in white heralded her appearance with a deafening scream. Clare reached out and immediately a glow issued forth from her. The lady in white screamed again and floated backwards away from Clare. The two women continued their slow walk towards Susan's room.

Clare noticed that the air grew thick, and it was difficult to breath, "You feel that Veronica?" "Yes, I think I'm going to choke," she coughed. Veronica put her hand on Clare's shoulder and let her guide them through the hall. It was as though they were walked through mud, the space seemed to be void of air, and each breath became more difficult, Veronica felt light headed. "Stay close to me" Clare said.

The din of noise was horrendous, by the time they reached Susan's room, but Clare maintained her concentration, the radiant light strong around her. Susan's body levitated, it had been lifted in mid-air, four black shadows slithered around her, one sat atop her in a strangle hold about her neck. "She's ours," it hissed at Clare.

Susan's arms hung like a rag doll below her body, Clare reached up and tried to grab her hand. If she could just get to her. Susan's body continued to rise out of her reach, Clare stood on the bed and reached towards the old woman who was nearly lifted to the twenty-foot ceiling. If she could just reach her hand. Suddenly, Veronica let go of Clare and screamed, the ghostly Mrs. Greene had grabbed her by the hair, and pulled her backward. Veronica was slammed against the wall, Clare was thrown off balance and fell to the floor, her light diminished.

In the dark, hands pushed at her, and she slid backwards to the end of the hall. Veronica screamed again as the ghostly Dr. Massey grabbed her arms, and the woman in white laid cold bony fingers on her face. Clare stood up, the light within her filled the hall, with a force she never knew she had, she reached out towards the apparitions, her hands closed in on their bodiless forms, and like a whiff of smoke they disappeared.

She went to Veronica and helped her up. Once again, they made their way to Susan's room, where she hung, suspended in mid-air, tormented by the evil filth that crawled over her, their hideous teeth bit into her, they swarmed in and out of her, blood streaked her gown. Clare climbed on the bed again and this time leaped up and grabbed her arm and pulled her body down onto the bed, she quickly shielded her with her own body, a flash of light shot out from her and pierced the hoard of tormentors. Their screams filled her head as they disappeared.

The light that came forth from Clare created a vacuum that enveloped the women, Susan cried out to her daughter, then fainted. Evil shadows exuded from her, and swirled around the room, they shrieked in rabid frustration. Clare reached out to them, a powerful flash filled the room and drove them back again, this time trapped in a brilliant explosion of light. Howls and screams filled the house and then silence. The room returned to normal, but she knew it wouldn't last long.

She quickly helped Susan out of the bed. It laughed, "So we meet again Clare," Perditus teased. She knew what it was, she felt its filth all over her. Memories of her parents' Arboretum that exploded in flames, the horrible fire that took her parents lives, flashed through her mind, she slowly turned around to face it. "Don't look at it Veronica," she said. Veronica hugged her mother close and shut her eyes. She lay on the bed in the fetal position wrapped around her mother.

Its' aura, a black void, pulled at her life force. The air in the room diminished, her throat tightened, and she choked. It's depth of darkness was like nothing Clare had ever encountered. "I know you," Clare rasped between coughs. Perditus backed slightly away from her, tilted its head to one side with an amused grin.

"Yes, we have met before, haven't we? "Gerry was such a nice guy," it teased. "But I just couldn't let him continue all that healing, he was a thief, wasn't he? He stole my souls from me you see. I worked hard for those miserable souls. Gerry had to go. I squeezed the life out of his puny heart, it was so easy, I so enjoyed that." Clare nearly fainted.

She remembered the moment it happened, she was in the greenhouse, they had planned an anniversary party that afternoon, Gerry was on his way home, the memory was as vivid now as the day it happened. The dreaded sensation that pierced her heart. She collapsed to the floor, little rubber bands tumbled out of the jar all over the concrete floor. Then it was behind her.

She remembered how it pointed to her parents' house, the explosion, the screams of her mother, the heat of the fire as it consumed everything, the broken glass of the greenhouse, the splinters of glass that exploded everywhere. She remembered it all. She remembered so clearly, things that for years she blocked from her memories, were so vivid, and now she relived the horror of it. She knew it wasn't an accident. It was all too coincidental for her husband's death and the tragic fire to happen all on the same day. Sadness crippled her. She was paralyzed with grief. She forgot where she was, what she was supposed to do.

Perditus climbed up the wall as it recanted all the gory details of that day Gerry died, it kept its eyes on Clare, it sized her up, confident she would be an easy victim of a merciless death. "You know you belong to me Clare, you don't have the power to cast me away. I on the other hand, have the power to end your life with torment and I will enjoy every minute of it. My little helpers have claimed and tormented the occupants of this pathetic dwelling place for centuries, after all they are like me, in that we have been consigned to this place, this place called earth.

Others like me, must wait until, well let's just say the right time presents itself. So, you see, we have nowhere to go but here, and all the time in the world. Torment is our job, it is what we are compelled to do by the one we serve. It's our work, our career, our task, our eternity."

"I, Perditus Odium, King of the Sons of Perdition!" it roared aloud. A hideous insane laugh followed. "In this case, I own the Daughters of Perdition, whom I have just recently claimed, perhaps you have heard of them, let me see, Lyla and Marla and well, I just tortured Cayla to death, she had a little too much good in her…. the loving daughters of Susan, so hateful to their mother. Do you really think you can come up against me?"

"What is that you ask? You don't know what a son or daughter of Perdition is? Surely, you must be joking! They are everywhere, I love them. Even I wouldn't do or say what they do. Not when it comes to the Creator. I'm not that stupid. But humankind, those brave arrogant souls who deny Him. Who turn their back on Him. I love those souls, they become mine in the blink of an eye. Just by that simple choice to say, "I don't believe there is a God," or better yet, my favorite,

"I don't believe in the Son of God." Especially those who were graced at birth, who sees the path to salvation, and instead flatly denies the existence of God, or denies God's gifts. Imagine the fun I have with them!! Perditus continued to pace the walls of Veronica's room, he circled Clare as a lion circles its prey all the while he spoke softly.

Clare regained her strength, she put her memories behind her and focused on the demon that slowly walked around her. She knew what it planned, it was going to come for her, it would be fast, it would try to take her as it took her husband and parents, but unlike them she could fight, and she was ready.

Clare's strength returned. She would stand her ground, she was no longer afraid, instead of fear she was filled with courage. A sense of courage that was calculated and determined to bring an end to this hideous creature. She was sure she could take it on, it didn't matter that it could kill her in the process, she was not afraid to die. An aggressive deadly force exuded from it and she felt it penetrate her mind and body her physical strength challenged.

She felt its power creep up her spine, it was all she could do to control it, from being consumed by it.

She felt pressure against her lungs as the air was slowly being squeezed from her again, it was playing with her, like a cat that toys with a mouse before it eats it, she became dizzy and her eyes blurred, it was during this split second that she realized she had one last chance before it would kill her.

She fell to her knees, her hands held in front of her exuding with every fiber of her being a powerful glow, but she knew she couldn't hold it much longer. It was just a matter of time, she choked and gasped for air that wasn't there, she fought for her life. Perditus came closer, each step stronger then the last, it had gained strength and confidence as it conversed with her.

"Look what I have done," Susan cried, tears streamed from her face, she watched in horror, as Perditus tormented Clare. "Can you ever forgive me Veronica," she wept. Veronica hugged her mother close and rocked her gently in her arms, "Of course I forgive you! I will always love you, always."

Michael appeared out of nowhere, Veronica and Susan were slumped over each other, he lifted them together, a light flashed, and they were in the back seat of Susan's Cadillac parked outside. He laid his hands upon their faces and said, "Sleep."

He turned back to the Manor and looked towards Susan's' bedroom window, he saw the flash of lights and heard the hideous screams. He walked back into the house and headed to the upper floor. Clare strained to hold up against the demon, finally she slumped over in a faint and crumpled to the ground. Michael entered the room just as Perditus was about to rip Clare's heart from her chest. "Get thee behind me ancient filth," he bellowed. Perditus spun around "Not this time," it seethed, and flew at Michael.

Michael rose up in fire and light unimaginable, a spear of huge dimensions long and deadly sharp held high over his head. Blinded, Perditus stumbled and fell at his feet and clawed at his legs, Michael stood over him, placed his foot on his neck, and leaned down on him, his spear poised for attack.

His face aglow and serene he said, "be gone," and pierced Perditus through. The floor of the room yawned open, a whirlpool of unimaginable depth rose up, Perditus and his minions, that for generations filled the Manor with hatred, despair and madness, were enveloped in a whirlpool of darkness. Michael touched his sword to the floor and sealed the portal, the air split with a deafening crack of lightning. The room returned to its earthly state, as did Michael.

Clare lay in a heap against the wall, she opened her eyes only to shield them with her hand from the brilliance that engulfed the room. She gasped in awe at the sight, of the one of intense radiance, a great being whose height measured easily as high as the twenty-foot ceiling. His face aglow and serene, hair streamed to his shoulders, wings unfurled and spread out the length of the room, he held in his hand a spear longer than any spear she had ever seen. He took her breath away.

They flew at each other in mid-air. He fought Perditus with ease, and then in a split second he lifted his spear above his head and pierced Perditus through. When the floor opened Clare covered her head and eyes, it felt as though her blood boiled, her skin and hair singed and blistered, "Oh God," she said as she crumpled over.

Chapter 24

Michael went to Clare and carried her out of the Manor and laid her in the truck. He touched her forehead and said, "forget." Veronica and Susan were still slumped over, asleep in the back seat of the Cadillac where Michael left them. He returned Veronica and her mother to the bedroom and laid them on the bed. They would sleep and remember nothing of this night, except that they loved each other. He and Clare would be on their way back to New York, before Veronica woke and discovered that her mother had passed away in the night.

The darkness of night gave way to the light of dawn, fresh dew covered the grass and beaded the wooden plant table and chairs strewn about. He sat on a lawn chair near the planting table, and waited for Clare to wake up. He looked up at the morning sky, fresh and new, it always reminded him of the first day of his existence.

This space was cleansed, he would move on from here to another place, soon. Clare would recognize him as the odd man that journeyed with her to Florida, complete with summer shorts, sandals and the tropical shirt she bought him.

Clare yawned, her body stiff from sleeping in a sitting position in the truck. She got out of the truck and stretched and stomped her legs to get the circulation going again. She looked around and saw Michael in a lawn chair amongst the clay pots and wilted plants. "Where's Veronica?" Clare asked as she walked up to him. "She is asleep in her mother's bed," Michael said. "When she awakens she will find her mother has passed away.

It's their time together, our work is done here." "What about her sisters?" Clare said. "Someone will be here on their behalf very soon," Michael said. "We have to go now, Clare."

Clare stood for a moment saddened at what Michael told her. She went inside the Manor, climbed the stairs to Susan's bedroom one last time and peeked in the room. She was tucked into her bed her face quiet and serene. Veronica lay next to her in a deep sleep. The room was warm and smelled like ozone, as though it had been struck by lightning.

The house was silent and peaceful. Clare sighed and silently went back downstairs. She remembered the house and its horrors, and she remembered the fight to get Susan cleansed of the evil that possessed her. Everything else was dim and foggy, but she knew she did what she was supposed to do. Michael was right, her work was done here.

She gathered a few water bottles and pieces of fruit from the kitchen and went out to meet Michael at the truck. She wanted to leave a note, perhaps she could come down or invite Veronica up to New York sometime. She didn't like the idea of leaving so suddenly. It just seemed rude. They were kindred spirits she, Veronica and Michael. For the first time in years she felt she had a family again.

Michael opened the truck door and got in, he waited patiently for Clare. "Okay then let's go home," she said as she backed out of the driveway. They drove through the night and except for gas and a bite to eat, they didn't stop until noon the next day. They made it back to New York in twenty-four hours driving straight through, only this time the drive was uneventful, and

Clare appeared to have tireless energy until they pulled into the Bristol Arboretum, her home sweet home. It was dark when they got there, and everything was quiet.

She turned the engine off and looked over at Michael. "Well we made it," she said. "Come on up and I'll make us something to eat." They got out of the truck and Michael carried Clare's bags upstairs to her home/office. He set the bags down and stood at the door.

"You're coming in, are you?" Clare said. "Time to go," Michael said. Clare turned to unlock the door, "well you can come in and have a cup of coffee and something to eat for the road, okay?" She opened the door and laid her bags down in the front room. It didn't dawn on her that Michael wouldn't follow her. She turned around, "Michael?" He was gone. He left as silently as he had arrived.

Her eyes welled with tears. She ran to the window and looked out, but it was too dark to see anyone. She called out to him to come back but knew he wouldn't answer her. She would miss him. She hoped he would come back. She looked out past the mercury vapor light at the entrance to her place, she thought she saw dull light in the distance, then it vanished.

She didn't want her time with Michael to end so abruptly, so much needed to be said, after all he never told her where he came from or where he was going. He just left. Friends don't do that to one another, friends don't disappear without a hug or handshake or a promise to be back again next year. She had nothing to remember him by, no phone number, address, he was just gone.

She was glad it was over and glad to be home and glad to be back to normal. For the first time in so many years she felt peace, she felt like her old self. That night, she slept without a nightmare, but rather she dreamt of Michael, only it didn't look like him, yet she was sure it was him. He stood on the precipice of a huge excavation, a hot wind blew around his ankle length robe and whipped around his legs, she saw a pyramid in the distance.

Michael stood like a Sentinel, his gaze set in the cavernous hole in the ground. Clare walked towards him, before she reached him she saw what looked like ancient ruins that had been unearthed, maybe by an archeologist, and then she woke up.

Chapter 25

Around five o'clock in the morning Veronica woke in her mothers' bed. The room was warm and smelled of ozone after a close lightning strike. She gathered herself together and sat up. There was softness to the balmy air.

The house felt quiet and peaceful. She sensed it was over. The last thing she remembered was holding her mother in the Cadillac. She turned to see Susan laid out on her bed completely still. Veronica reached over to wake her mother, her arm was cold to the touch. She came around to Susan's side of the bed and tried to wake her. A crumpled piece of paper peeked out of her fist, it was tattered, as though it had been around for some time.

Veronica,

All these years I held so much bitterness in my heart, I don't know why. Please forgive me, I love you.

Veronica sat for a moment on her mother's bed holding her hand. It was over, and she had made peace with her mother here at the very end. She hoped she could do the same with her sisters. She would call them in the morning. Veronica kissed her mother one last time and gently covered her body with the bed sheet. She went downstairs and called the sheriff's office and reported Susan's death.

The Sheriff's deputy and coroner arrived fifteen minutes later. After an initial conversation with the sheriff and coroner who pronounced her mother dead of natural causes, Veronica watched as they zipped Susan's body into a body bag, then placed her body in the coroner's truck and with red lights flashing, it silently drove away to the Marion Funeral Home.

She knew she had to call her sisters but wasn't sure where they were. She remembered that Cayla was coming home soon, so she decided to call her first, to see if she was home yet. She locked up Susan's house and went back to her place. She would wait until later in the week to try to reach Marla and Lyla, according to what her mother told her, they who were not due home from the fishing trip for a few more days.

She couldn't find any phone numbers for anyone who knew where her sisters were. She realized that she would just have to wait until they got home, to make any funeral arrangements for their mother.

It was four o'clock in the afternoon when the sheriff deputy drove up her driveway. They told her that Cayla's body was at the airport in Jacksonville. The next of kin, Cayla's husband, had asked them to notify Veronica and that he would have her body sent to the Marion Funeral Home. Before Veronica could respond the Sheriff's Deputy also told her that there had been a terrible storm off the coast of the Bahamas last night, and a few of the sailing vessels were destroyed.

The Sheriff held a report from the Miami Port Authorities that listed guests of the Southern Winds, one of the Sloops that sunk. Everyone was found and accounted for except Lyla and Marla Ginsburg. "The vessel and your sisters, perished, their bodies were never recovered," the deputy said. He extended his hand to Veronica and said, "we are very sorry for your loss."

Veronica and Bob Wythe, Cayla's husband, met at the funeral home when Cayla's body arrived from the airport. Her daughter wouldn't arrive for another day. There was much to be done to prepare for the funeral.

They decided that Cayla, her sisters and mother would all be remembered in the same service.

The killer storm went national, and the local news carried the news about the Ginsburg family on the front pages of the Marion Dispatch Newspaper. For several days newspaper reporters called to interview Veronica on the tragic loss of her sisters and mother. Veronica ignored the ringing phone and messages. Veronica listened to the Reverend James Franklin extend his sincere sympathies to the family, then a series of distant relatives that Veronica hadn't seen in over twenty years, came forward and spoke about their times with her sisters and mother. The service went on for close to two hours. The bodies of Susan and Cayla were buried in the Marion County Cemetery. Several months later, two plaques that Veronica ordered for Lyla and Marla were placed next to their parents' gravestones.

Veronica inherited Wedgewood Manor. She decided she would have an auction and then sell the place. Three weeks after the auction a fire broke out, and the house burned to the ground. The County Fire Chief could find no evidence of foul play and concluded that the fire was due to old electrical wiring.

Forty days after the funeral, and after Veronica finished work in the gardens, to prepare for the Master Gardeners meeting the next day, she sat down on the back deck with a glass of tea. As the evening sun went behind the tops of the trees Veronica noticed a woman in one of the gardens, she recognized her mother immediately. She stood up and just as she was about to call out to her, the woman faded into the evening light. Susan had come to say goodbye. Veronica walked through the garden hopeful that she would see her again, perhaps her sisters, were here too. But the gardens gave way to a gentle breeze that blew through the trees and the whisper of leaves as invisible swirls of wind played through them.

The day faded to twilight. Whippoorwills called to one another and the neighbor's guinea hens chattered noisily as they settled into the trees for the night. The evening air lifted the scent of gardenias and roses and floated their fragrance through the gardens. What a wonderful way to end this day," Veronica thought to herself, "a fragrance to remember you by mother." She stood for a few minutes longer, she wished she could collect the heady fragrance in the air and put it in a bottle.

She watched the fireflies randomly light up the darkness. "This moment," she thought, "should last forever."

Chapter 26
Perditus Odium

"I reap the souls of the sons and daughters of Perdition. I am Perditus Odium, foul angel of darkness. I claim lost souls, spiritually ruined, marvelously unrepentant, whose lives are mine to destroy and bring into eternal damnation and eternal punishment not necessarily after death, many I taunt for a lifetime or until I snuff out their lives with physical destruction and misery."

"But alas, I sit here in this frigid darkness. I wait. It's just a matter of time before I will arise again and pick up where I left off. The wait to inflict pain and suffering is an easy wait. Humankind, that pathetic fragile host that bears a dim light. Mankind. So predictable in its cycle of wars, depravity, cruelty, hate, death, death, and death. Such delicious misery is mine to inflict."

"So I, Perditus, waits. Always I arise, always I destroy, *always* I take delight in piercing the bodies and souls of mankind with affliction and temptation. The harvest is great for those who succumb to me, great Angel of Darkness that I am. I reap. I pluck them from eternal salvation. So easy. I place my disguise, lies, and temptations upon the table of human appetite. I fish for them as fish in a barrel, I gather *my* souls. It is a matter of time before I rise again."

"Clare," Perditus hissed aloud. How many millennia have past, how many "Clares" have I destroyed. Well, perhaps not their souls but certainly I make sure they are consumed with pain and suffering right up to their last breath. I hate them most of all. Envy roars in me for the light that shines bright in them, that is my light and I will have it back!" The person Clare, escaped him again. There would be no next time.

He thought back to the time she was born, she surprised him that day when she saw him and announced to her mother that there was a 'black animal' in the kitchen. "Imagine that, she called *me* an animal. I should have been rid of her in the fire that killed her parents and again at the Manor where I almost finished her off before *He* showed up and banished me. A special suffering awaits Clare," mused Perditus. "Are you afraid? You should be," he softly hissed to himself.

Perditus recalled passed victories; the wars. The greatest feats of all time, entire nations compelled to murder each other. So much suffering. Now a godless age has taken hold upon the earth. Nations award greed, hedonism and death *especially death* as a blessing upon each other, their own kind, their unborn, the young in the bloom of their lives, and the very old. Perditus smiled at the thought of those whose god is human appetite. Aah, just a matter of time, I'll be back. "Are you afraid? You should be." Perditus cackled.

In the dark and silent frigid space, banished by Michael that great defender of men, his once beloved brother, Perditus waits. For it is just a matter of time before humans will choose darkness over light again. "It only takes a small nudge to tempt them," Perditus boasted to himself. "Are you afraid? You should be."

■■

Coming Soon

The Man from Cairo

By

Anne Veronica Hierholzer Conover

Copyright 2018©AnneVeronicaHierholzerConover

Mohammad Hiyad hurried through the early morning crowd of buyers and sellars in the marketplace. He held something wrapped in cloth close to his chest. He looked furtively from side to side wary of any strangers who might try to take his possession from him.

He zig-zagged through the crowd, it seemed an eternity just to get to the outskirts of the city, sweat trickled down his face.

The heat of the day intensified and bore into his back as he pressed on through the crowd. He hurried on. He hoped to be back before the sun set. He had to bury his father, and the family awaited his return to make the necessary arrangements. But this was more important, his father told him so on his death bed. He could not put off the return of the parcel he held close to his chest and that now pulsed like a beating heart.

When he reached the outskirts of the city he broke into a steady jog towards the excavation site. He would worry about how to get the artifact into the temple when he got there. The temple site loomed in the distance, signs pointed the way for tourists. He never let up and through the heat of the afternoon he pressed forward, he felt fear chase him like a lion.

It was late in the afternoon when he finally arrived, exhausted and covered in sand and road dust, he slowed to a walk as to not draw attention to himself. It was near closing time and the tourists were few. He hid behind a large temple stone that lay on its side outside the temple entrance. The site would close an hour before dark, he would have enough time to replace the object he held in the cloth and get out of the temple. The city lights of Cairo would guide him back home.

He waited, hidden from the tourists and the guards who waited to lock up the doors to the entrance. It didn't matter that the doors would be locked. He had a key. Soon the guards locked up and left for the night. Hiyad had less than thirty minutes to replace the artifact that his father gave him on his death bed.

The artifact began to tremble in his arms. He had to be quick, he had to get it back in the Magicians chest. He had a key for that too. He ran to the doors unlocked them and quickly scurried into the main temple. He ran through the large open space dotted with statues and walls covered in hieroglyphs. He turned left into a corridor that was blocked by a heavy metal door, he unlocked it and pushed hard to open it, the door had been locked for over thirty years, by his own father. Not since that fateful day when his father stole the artifact had the door been open. The light of day waned, and dark shadows grew in the corners of the temple.

Hiyad entered the Magicians Chambers, his father warned him not to hesitate, or to look about the room and to believe nothing of what he thought he saw or heard.

Just find the Magicians Chest, the one with a staff and cobra carved into the lid.

There were no windows in the Magicians Chambers, only the dim light that came from the door that he left ajar, of the oncoming twilight. The chest was set upon a pedestal about four feet in height. A hum came from it, and there was a vibration that buzzed through his hands as Hiyad struggled to open the chest with the key. He obeyed his father and ignored the sound and the vibration of the chest as he tried to unlock it, and he ignored the growing pulse of the artifact in the cloth.

He opened the chest and a brilliant light shone forth, the sound of timbrels and flutes floated out of it, singing voices trilled about the room. He picked up the artifact and placed it in the blinding light of the chest and quickly slammed it shut. His hands shook as he locked the chest. For a brief second, it felt as though the air and been sucked out of the room.

Hiyad turned and ran out the door of the Magicians Chambers. He continued to run past the statues and hieroglyphs and out the main door. Fear had swallowed him up, and in his panic, he forgot to lock the doors. He didn't remember that he forgot to lock the doors the next day, or the day after that.

Hiyad and his family buried his father the next day. He still had to clean out his fathers' office at the university. He thought that since there were so many artifacts that he would donate them all to the Egyptian Museum of Antiquities, after all they belonged to Egypt. He dressed in his best suit, the one like his father's suit, the one he wore to work every day. He drove his father's truck to the university such that he could pack up all the personal affects that belonged to his father and now belonged to him.

He was early, as the Museum movers were coming in a few hours and he wanted to make sure that he got to his father's office, before they did. He and several friends drove up to the entrance of the university School of Egyptology, he parked in his father's parking space. It was close enough to the school such that boxes would not have to be carried too far.

Hiyad felt sad upon entering his father's office. He had visited many times, everything was so familiar, his fathers' presence was in every book, artifact, and piece of furniture in the office space. It was all so familiar. In the center of the room were boxes taped up and marked with the family name written on them. Among the boxes was an unwrapped pedestal. Hiyad recognized it immediately. A flash of memory overcame him, and he became afraid. Atop the pedestal was the box with the carved staff and cobra etched into it. The one he left in the Temple not long ago. There was no way the box was supposed to be in the office and he wondered who brought it out of the Magicians Chambers. How would they know to bring it here to his father's office? How did they get in? Then he remembered how he rushed out of the Temple, and he wondered did he forget to lock the room? To his horror, he remembered that he forgot to lock the Magicians Chamber, and the interior doors were left unlocked as well. A hum issued forth from the wooden box upon the pedestal, but no one heard it except Hiyad. He had to get it back to the Temple.

    The men carried all the boxes out to the truck, they carried the pedestal and carved wooden box that only Hiyad could hear hum. They drove the truck out to Hiyad's house where they unloaded all the artifacts that belonged to his father and that were to be kept in the family. Tomorrow Hiyad would drive out to the Temple and put the carved wooden box back in the Magicians' Chambers, and this time he wouldn't forget to lock the doors on the way out.

Made in the USA
Middletown, DE
28 February 2018